MURDER IN ICE

Margot Peters

with

Leslie DeMuth and Steve Bower

Also by Margot Peters

Charlotte Brontë: Style in the Novel
Unquiet Soul: A Biography of Charlotte Brontë
Bernard Shaw and the Actresses
Mrs Pat: The Life of Mrs Patrick Campbell.
The House of Barrymore
May Sarton: A Biography
Wild Justice (as Margret Pierce)
Design for Living: Alfred Lunt and Lynn Fontanne
Summers: A True Love Story
Lorine Niedecker: A Poet's Life
Exorcising Emma: A Memoir

I gratefully acknowledge:

- Kevin Lehner, who dreamed up the real Icehenge and confided to me the secrets of its construction
- Leann Lehner, for kindly critiquing the manuscript
- Claire Peters, for her remarkable copy-editing skills
- Bill Stork, DVM, who gave me the background to create Dr. Smitty Barker and his methods
- Eli Wiedel, photographer, for permission to use his stunning photograph of Icehenge
- Barry Luce and Tom Boyks, for graciously consenting to my using their cleverly altered names
- Bob Cradock, Mac expert and book stylist
- Peter Jordan, who, generously as always, put up with the throes of my thirteenth book
- Most especially, Leslie DeMuth and Steve Bower: co-conspirators, plotters, critics, and technical advisors

CHAPTER ONE

"Whose bright idea was it to kick this off at six a.m.?" grumbled city councilman Chet Newman, stamping his boots on rough ice.

"The sun's," replied Wilkie Steeves more shortly than he intended but, after all, he hadn't had the first cup of the day. "In this year of grace 1980 it happens to rise on February second at 7:20."

Councilwoman Diane Frye nudged the City Manager's arm in sympathy. "Always a critic," she breathed through layers of scarf.

"Town's crawling with them."

Then he mentally cancelled his words. Not a bad town, Mills Lake. Its support for the finer things in life like ice fishing and two local breweries struck him as enlightened. And the town could certainly crank up the community spirit. When downtown storefronts went vacant, other businesses moved in. When causes needed support, the Chamber, EMS, Main Street Program, police department, tavern owners—even the new Arts Alliance—stepped up big-time.

So now, as people gathered on the frozen lake, he smiled with reasonable benevolence as he fumbled in his parka for his speech. Some residents pulled bundled children on sleds or bumped them in strollers over snowmobile ruts. Many clutched thermoses of hot coffee—or brandy—to ward off the nine degree chill, though a posse of teenagers slapping a puck across the pitted ice were wearing shorts. Oddly, the cold and dark seemed to excite the crowd. Folks back-slapped friends, stamped their feet in anticipation, sent up a cheer for the Green Bay Packers due to meet the detested Chicago Bears the following day, applauded drag-car hero Ken Madson as he braked his Polaris to a snow-spitting stop.

Who *had* suggested launching this year's Winter Carnival at dawn, wondered Steeves. Typically the festival kicked off at nine Saturday morning with the ice fisheree, followed by the crowning of the Winter King and Queen, hayrides, ice hockey competitions, the IditerDad race in the Commons, and the judging of the quite spectacular ice sculptures that had been carved by area artists Friday

1

evening as they hoped for a long freeze. The firing of grills downtown for a "Rib-Off" and a local brewery's lavish distribution of free beer rounded off the popular event on a high level of cheer.

Steeves slapped his gloves. Of course he knew whose idea it had been. Devon Lang, the creative brain behind what he swore would be a spectacular addition to the Carnival, had urged unveiling "Icehenge" at dawn—arguing there'd be state-wide, even national, interest. And he'd been right. The City Manager's phone had been jumping with calls from CBS and NBC as well as from media statewide. Looking round, he saw that TV crews outnumbered local photographers as they positioned their equipment to capture the sun's first rays striking the ice structure inspired by England's Druidic Stonehenge.

As the dark dissolved, the men responsible for Icehenge— Devon Bond, Quinn Hale, Bill Byrd and his son Cal— high-fived each other in anticipation. Sawing huge slabs of ice out of the lake had been a challenge, but erecting the seven-foot uprights and hoisting fourteen lintel blocks weighing 200 pounds each to top them had tested their stamina to the limits. Creating Icehenge had been twice the challenge because, as men with day jobs, they'd mostly had to cut and assemble the blocks after dark with only headlights from Bond's Cherokee illuminating their work.

"Though working in the dark's really an advantage," Hale had insisted. "Do we really want the *Leader* scooping our Masterpiece"—his voice capitalized the first letter—"before the opening?"

"Not that we can hide it when it's sitting out there in full view during the day. That's why I wanted it at the end of Coolidge, Quinn. More private."

Quinn shook his head. "Having it off Bartel's is going to give us fifty times more exposure. Don't tell me that's not what you want."

Bill Byrd was the only man tall and strong enough to singly heave a lintel atop the columns with rope and pulley; he had gloomily predicted that Icehenge would be trashed by vandals before they unveiled it. A kind man, he kept his pessimism to himself. Especially he didn't want to discourage his seventeen-year-old son, who was thrilled to be involved.

"Look at that sky, guys," said Devon, "and forget the big scene of first rays striking old Henge."

They looked. Behind a scrim of cloud a cranky sun was hauling itself out of bed as though seriously resenting being awakened.

"Shit," said Quinn, taking a fortifying nip from his flask. "She looks like a jilted bride."

Wilkie Steeves adjusted the mic pinned to his collar and raised a hand to greet the crowd. Although he had no enthusiasm for public speaking, he'd pushed it as one of his qualifications for city manager.

"Welcome to the Mills Lake fifth Winter Carnival." Staring at his notes, he discovered it was still too dark to read a word he'd written. He stuffed the paper into his parka and forged on. "Maybe you're asking why your City Manager is kicking off this year's event instead of Main Street and the Chamber of Commerce, the people who organized it. Well, I'm asking too." He paused, acknowledging the laugh.

"We're here this morning to unveil a highly unusual work of art crafted by three—four actually—local men in honor of the event. They are Devon Bond, Quinn Hale, Bill Byrd, and Bill's son Cal. Let's give them all a hand!" He led the applause, pounding together thick leather gloves. "And now—" he turned hopefully to the east— "as the old song goes: 'Here comes the sun!'"

Heads swiveled and a sigh riffled through the crowd like an arctic wind. No dazzling rays glinting off Icehenge but the subdued light of a sun behind clouds: a morose sun, a mopey sun, a bashful sun. Still, the dark was dissolving and the familiar shapes of boathouses, fishing shacks, lake homes and faces were beginning to emerge. Above their heads, excusing themselves from the celebration, five black crows flapped slowly over the lake, as though to say we seek better entertainment—and roadkill— elsewhere.

But then the cloud cover suddenly broke and, as they watched, the monumental "Icehenge" began to glow dimly along its edges, then to discreetly brighten as light ventured across its lintels and down its columns. Gradually people started to clap, then cheer, then surge toward the structure they could now almost see.

TV cameras closed in as at last the Henge began to glow with a light that some, looking back, would call "mystic" and others "sinister."

Only seconds later a five-year-old-boy yanked at his mother's parka sleeve. He was pointing and shouting and jumping up and down.

"Mommy, Mommy, look! See there, in that ice thingy. *It looks like a lady!*"

CHAPTER TWO

Tillie released her very large suitcase to the man who greeted her at the door.

"Barry Boycks, concierge."

"Matilda Roth Hamilton," she said, sticking out her hand. Because he was holding both door and suitcase, he was forced to set her case down before he could offer his. Looking rather oppressed by her three names, he waved her into a formal hall dominated by a magnificent oak staircase that curved steeply upward.

"Welcome, Matilda. Ever been to Wisconsin?" Standard question.

"No, but looking forward to my stay." Standard answer. Tillie smothered a yawn. She'd caught the red-eye from La Guardia after a shockingly late night celebrating the promotion of her friend Kathryn Meadows to assistant editor of *Art World*. Now, to underline her looking forwardness, she clasped her hands and nodded approval at the tiled fireplace, an absurdly ornate chandelier, two high-backed velvet chairs, an oil lamp converted to electricity, and a sideboard massive as two coffins. Giving up all hope of TV, she turned to the staircase, longing only to haul herself up it and flop into the advertised four-poster king.

"No elevator," said Boycks, so unnecessarily that she giggled through her yawns. Upstairs, he threw open a door, motioned her inside with a flourish.

Long live Queen Victoria! Under a purple-velvet canopy dripping tassels stood a four-poster so lofty that a step-stool had been provided to help her vault into bed. She took in a tiled fireplace with a grate the size of a mailing envelope, a washstand with flowered china pitcher and bowl, lace curtains muffling three tall windows. And Teddy bears. *Were* teddy bears really Victorian? she wondered. She must research the matter.

"Bathroom in here."

Looking in, she sent up a prayer of thanks to twentieth century plumbing, then joined Boycks in front of the miniscule fireplace. "We don't allow fires in rooms," he said seriously, "so don't plan on a wienie roast or anything."

"And all those marshmallows for S'mores in my suitcase." She looked again at his card and then at him. A neutral man, an inch or two taller than she. Trim, contained. Face bland as a priest's. Pale green eyes; short-clipped coppery hair; matching coppery beard trimmed meticulously close to the jaw. Black fine-waled corduroy jacket, striped green and black waistcoat, pink ascot: something of a dude. Would he know the man she'd come to interview? Catching his watchful eyes on her, she decided that Barry Boycks probably knew everyone and everything in town.

"As I said on the phone, I'm here til next Saturday. I don't think I told you, but I'm doing a magazine piece on a local artist, Dexter Hoyt. Do you know him?"

Boycks shrugged, face still idling in neutral. "Hoyt's known in Mills Lake. I'm surprised he's known anywhere else."

"Maybe he isn't," said Tillie. "But that's about to change."

CHAPTER THREE

Tillie had booked an interview with Dexter Hoyt that afternoon. Hitching her briefcase over the shoulder of her "gently used" black coat with fox-fur collar (guilt! guilt! but after all the fox had not been killed for *her*), she set out, directions clutched in her gloved hand. Drifts three-feet tall, she noted, and cold as grandma's ice box—though not as perishing as New York with a January wind off the East River.

Mentally she snapped photos of the downtown as she hurried along. A park with many trees, a bandstand and benches. A few skaters circling a Currier and Ives rink. Mom-and-pop restaurant facing the park, a strange copper cone peaking its roof. A nineteenth-century yellow brick building announcing itself as Bistro Dining and Opera House Antiques. Could it have been the town's old opera house? Oh, good guess, Tillie!

Where, she wondered, is that lake with mills the town was named for?

She passed a BP station, a church advertising that "God Is Still Speaking," and found Coolidge Street. An old street, she saw immediately, defined by old trees, their lofty branches gloved in white. Big, porchy Victorian-era houses, a few newer ones sandwiched in between. Not new-new, she corrected herself: 1960s at the latest.

Coolidge Street turned out to be four blocks long. She walked until, at the end of block three, she finally got a glimpse of lake at the bottom of a steep hill. There it was: white, frozen, its icy expanse oddly punctuated by black huts as though an invading army of miniature enemies were camping out before they attacked. She shook her head; must ask Boycks the concierge about those huts. But where was 515 and how could she possibly have missed it?

Retracing her steps, she spotted what she'd missed before: a venerable carriage house tucked between two upscale Victorians at the end of a long drive. Could this be it? She walked up the drive. On the third ring she decided either that she had the wrong house or that Dexter Hoyt was ignoring their appointment. But then as she was pushing aside a vine screening a broken window stuffed with rags, the front door flew open. A man of medium height and any age between thirty and forty-five glared at her from beneath a flop of black hair forked by a silver streak. She thought of lightning splitting a black stormy sky.

"Well?"

"Well, yes," she said incisively, extending her hand. "Matilda Roth Hamilton and I believe we have an appointment." She deliberately pushed back a coat sleeve and pointed at her watch— "at two p.m."

He massaged his jaw with thumb and forefinger, struggling to place her. Finally he said: "Hold on a minute. Are you *Art World?*"

"Exactly."

"Sorry, sorry, sorry. Please come in."

She followed him into a large cold space reeking of turpentine and chaotic with palettes, rags, canvases, brushes, and easels. It also seemed to be stuffed with antiques, though on second look she dismissed most of the chaos as junkyard finds. Dexter Hoyt's studio was a pack-rat's dream. Too bad she was not a pack-rat.

Still in her coat and shivering, she looked about for a stove, a fireplace, even an electric heater. Nothing. Then she saw it and stopped shivering. Almost, she crossed herself. Propped against an easel, stood "Woman with Snake."

Amazing. Here, in front of her, in an unknown artist's pad in nowhere Mills Lake, Wisconsin, was the badly-reproduced painting that a year ago had arrow-sped from the pages of an obscure Wisconsin magazine to bury itself in her heart.

She approached it, hissing in admiration.

"I had no idea, *no idea at all.*" She turned to him, eyes shining. "My god, the brushwork, the palate, the textures! I don't have words."

"Thanks."

Had he really heard her? He had wandered off to a bank of windows at the rear of the studio. Following him, peering over his shoulder, she saw a winter garden scored with trellises and stakes and crisscrossed by yellow follow-the-dots dog pee.

Was a brief thanks all she was going to get for an article that could make his reputation? He seemed hardly conscious of her presence. Oh, she'd had a premonition, all right. As Northwest flight 496 droned over frozen Pennsylvania, Ohio, and Michigan and finally descended over even more deeply frozen Wisconsin, she'd felt every precious New York link she'd forged snapping free. Who in this godforsaken wasteland could possibly care about art? What could she possibly extract from it of value?

She pulled herself together. "This garden, is it a particular inspiration to you?"

"It was." He seemed to recall he had a visitor. "Care to have a seat, uh, Matilda—"

"Tillie, please." She gave him what she hoped—and truly was— a warm and reverent smile.

He nodded and smiled at her for the first time, a surprisingly sweet smile, like a boy's. Suddenly she felt she might win him over.

Locating one of the less cluttered chairs, she pulled out notebook and pen. "Shall we dive right in? I may use a tape-recorder later, but I have to admit I hate all the transcribing. So notes for now?"

"Fine with me. Preferable, in fact. I hate talking into those damn recorder things. Your voice never comes out as your own."

She drew a deep breath. "I can't tell you how excited I am to be here, talking with you, Mr. Hoyt. There are so many things I want to ask you, but can we start with 'Woman with Snake'? I'm curious. For example, did you use a model? Because the woman: she's real but, if you understand me, not real."

"Isn't that the point?"

"Please don't think I'm hung up on realism. I love the way your work draws the viewer into its own particular never-never land."

He frowned. "I should offer you something," he said vaguely. Had he taken in what she'd just said? "Tea? Coffee? The cheap drunk's box wine?"

9

"Please don't bother," she said, but he was already on his feet and she wanted to be polite "All right then, tea for me."

Am I ever going to pin down this guy to an interview?

A kettle shrieked; eventually he returned carrying two steaming mugs and set them down with a slosh on a stack of what looked like unpaid bills. Her hand went automatically for Kleenex to sop up the mess, but stopped. Don't be *conventional*, she scolded herself, *this is an artist.* Instead she sank her voice to hushed reverence. "Can we please talk about 'Woman with Snake?'"

"Don't see why not, though it's no favorite of mine."

"Then let's start with the when, the where, the what and the why."

His fingers raked his black hair into furrows; she remembered inconsequentially that he'd been raised on a farm.

"The when's easy. I finished it last year."

"So in 1979 . . . "

"Complication. *I never really finish a painting.*"

"Ah!" She jotted in her notebook, underlining *never finish* twice. "Fascinating! Then how about the 'where?'"

He leaned forward, hands gripping heavy thighs. "Is the where important?"

"I believe it is, yes."

"My studio has windows"—he jerked a thumb over his shoulder—"ergo I have a view. When I look out these windows I see a back yard with a garden. That's the 'where.'"

Tillie smiled. "So there *was* a snake in this garden."

His eyebrows shot up. "You say you're not hung up on realism, yet now you're suggesting a real snake?"

"That was a very small joke. Let's go on to the 'what.' I'm guessing you painted an actual woman."

"Look, she was just a neighbor—okay? Once in a while I'd see her in her back yard gardening or raking or stuff. She never sat for me, I never asked her to. I couldn't afford to, for starters. If you can't see that 'Woman with Snake' is a *vision,* not a portrait, Matilda-all-your-names, maybe you're not the person to be interviewing me."

She did not hurl her notebook at his head; after all he was her own undiscovered genius. Instead she leaned forward with a smile. "Then let's talk about your *vision*, Mr. Hoyt. Let's talk about why a woman digging in her garden inspired you."

Hoyt frowned into his tea mug without answering.

"Did you, for example, use her in other paintings? Not herself, of course, but your *vision* of her?"

"Damned if I know," he said and belched.

If I *did* catch that next plane to New York, she thought, I could be 200 miles away from this lout tomorrow. Then, remembering her rather generous advance from *Art World,* she pressed on. "Can you tell me what about her grabbed your artistic imagination?"

Hoyt jumped to his feet and began to pace.

"Proximity, ever heard of it? Well, everything in life is proximity. Rembrandt didn't go scouring for models, he used his cleaning lady or his mistress or even his wife. Statistics show that seventy-eight per cent of married couples have found their partners within a radius of two miles. This woman happened to live next door. Look, can we drop the subject because I'm beginning to think, Matilda et cetera, that you haven't a clue—"

Tillie studied Hoyt for a count of ten, then methodically began gathering together her notebooks, binders and pens. Clearly he was hopeless. She zipped shut her briefcase.

"Mr. Hoyt, I simply don't understand your obstructive and insulting attitude. You signed a contract with *Art World* for this article."

He thrust his fists into his pockets and glared at her from under the flop of silver-streaked hair.

"And *you* are being incredibly insensitive."

"*I*? Insensitive?" She stared at him open-mouthed.

"You must have seen it on TV or in the papers."

"Seen what? Mr. Hoyt, please give me a break. I don't have a clue what you're talking about for the simple reason I only arrived in Mills Lake three hours ago."

He resumed pacing, finally halting at that bank of windows that marched along the rear of the studio. Northern light, she remembered; all artists need northern light. (And female inspiration?)

"Then let me inform you. Last week on February second—nine days ago, to be exact—the town rolled out its annual three days of tasteless debauch known as the Winter Carnival. This year our problematic City Manager kicked off the carnival at the ungodly hour of six a.m. with the unveiling of a massive but sadly crude ice sculpture christened "Icehenge." You know: Stonehenge, Druids, the Solstice—all that pagan crap. I went down to the lake out of curiosity; it was dark and cold as hell. After an eternity, the sun finally managed to put in an appearance. And there it was."

Tillie set down her briefcase. "Icehenge, you mean."

"Icehenge, yes. And something unexpected."

"Like what?"

"A woman. Frozen into one of those columns."

"My god."

"I couldn't stay to look so I headed back up the hill. I can't believe you didn't know, I was sure that's why you came to interview me today. It's been all over TV."

"Not *my* TV, Mr. Hoyt. Do they know the woman's identity?"

"They know, all right. " He jerked a thumb at the painting Tillie most admired. "The Henge woman was my woman through the window, my backyard neighbor, my Ceres of the garden. My vision—or what was left of her."

"How terrible! I'm so sorry."

"You still don't understand. *The whole town thinks I murdered her.*"

CHAPTER FOUR

"If you don't call a public session, Council's gonna call it for you."

Wilk Steeves camouflaged his dislike of Chet Newman with a yawn behind his hand. Since the discovery of "Our Lady of the Ice"—as everybody was calling the remains of the unfortunate Liz Barker—Newman had been buzzing round him like a horse fly.

"To tell the Council what, exactly? That we've been working with local police and Madison forensic teams since day one and still don't have a clue? That a month in the water has obliterated all traces of cause of death and possible weapon? That fragments of clothing removed from the body reveal exactly nothing?" He shifted into higher gear. "That even the coroner's statement that she was dead before she went into the water is, in his own words, guesswork? That it's all of seven days, including two Sundays, since it happened? So tell me, Chet: what kind of session does Council have in mind?"

"You're not getting the mood of the town, Wilk. Folks are fixated on the murder and nobody's happy with what's been done. Correction: *not been done.*"

Steeves reared up behind his vast desk. "Hold it right there, Chet. First: I know the mood of the town like I know my right hand. Second: we still don't know Liz Barker was murdered."

"What, she just walks into the lake and drowns herself! Get real."

"I'm quite real, thanks for your concern. And I know something you apparently don't." He leaned forward and planted his fists on his desk. "That a case can take months—years—to crack. That no public yammering's going to push solid police work one inch nearer the solution. Go ahead, Chet, call a meeting. You can announce that the police are doing everything in their power to solve this crime. Then you can say, 'Th-a-a-t's all, folks.'"

Steeves wished he felt as confident as his words.

On impulse, he'd phoned Devon Bond two days ago, leaving a message that he wanted to talk with him. Bond had replied, they'd set a date. Now Devon walked in on Newman's exit and took the indicated chair. He did not look happy.

"Sorry to drag you down here, Mr. Bond. You've been totally co-operative and I know how much Chief Sherpinski appreciates that."

"I don't see what else I could be, City Manager, under the circumstances."

"Wilk's the name. Now, as I understand it, the police investigation keeps coming back to one thing: Icehenge."

"Wish I'd never dreamed up the damn thing!"

"Point taken. As you know, I'm not the law, so this is strictly between you and me. So for my own peace of mind, I'd appreciate your walking me through the Icehenge process. The Henge was your idea, right?"

"It was. Though when I mentioned it to my buddies, they jumped right in."

"You began it when?"

Devon unzipped his parka and Steve noted that his neck was fiery-red. Allergies? Sun lamp? Fear?

"I drew up the plans last fall, took quite a bit of geometry, actually."

"I'd like to hear about that some day."

"Glad to oblige. Anyway, I got two other guys excited about the idea. Then we had to wait for a solid freeze. *And* wait. Finally we got it early January."

Steeves nodded. He remembered the day the DNR had announced that ice on Mills Lake was a solid three inches only because a week before he'd driven his Jimmy onto the ice, cut a hole and dropped a line.

"We had to work pretty fast—we didn't have that much time before Carnival. Actually, I don't know how we did it. My back's still on the rack."

"So you worked what—a couple of weekends?"

"Just one, actually. Mainly we worked at night."

14

"I didn't realize that." Steeves frowned at his desk blotter, then looked up at Bond, eyes narrowed. "What I can't figure our is how you could possibly see what you were doing."

"I had my doubts too—um, Wilk—but it worked. I'd drive my Cherokee onto the lake at Bartel's Beach and we'd work in the headlights. One night Bill Byrd brought his truck, so we had stereo, so to speak."

"And you worked how many nights?"

"Let's see." The fire had spread into Devon's face, scorching the skin over his high cheekbones "Okay, we started late January—"

"Can you be more specific?"

Devon shot him a wounded look. "Look, City Manager, the police have already grilled me about this."

"But I'd appreciate it if you'd go over it again for me. "

"Right," he said in a resigned kind of way. "I'm pretty sure it was a Sunday—you got a calendar there?"

Steeves reached for his desk calendar. "Both twenty and twenty-seven were Sundays."

"Twenty-seven's correct. And we only finished a couple of days before Carnival, so"—Devon ticked off his fingers and shook his head in wonderment—"I can't believe we did it in six."

Steeves came around his desk, balanced on the edge, loomed over Bond.

"The police have asked you this, I know. *But at any time were you aware you were cutting something besides ice?"*

Bond swallowed hard. "I swear we weren't. You can ask the others—"

"They've been asked."

"Well, I can't swear to what *they* saw, but all I saw was ice."

"Did you ever work without headlights?"

"How could we?"

Steeves glanced at a note he'd extracted from a pocket. "On February first the moon was full."

Devon frowned, snapped his fingers with a pop that didn't come off.

"I remember now. Okay, something weird came over us when we realized we'd virtually finished the Henge. It was almost like a vision, a tribal vision. Suddenly we knew we had to finish the job by moonlight. Like the Druids finished Stonehenge."

Steeves looked even more thoughtful.

"So, yeah, the moon was full. Why?"

"Because I—not to mention the MLPD—am trying to nail down a time when you could be cutting ice yet *unaware you were also cutting through a body*. And I can only see it happening the night you doused your headlights because of the full moon."

CHAPTER FIVE

A sign surmounting the gate announced that these Tower Street premises were under surveillance by 24/7SECUR. Tillie shrugged. Most art collectors (in her admittedly brief experience) had such defenseless defenses. And when Adam Quick cracked his door, she was unsurprised again. Collectors seemed to live in terror of being robbed.

"Matilda Roth Hamilton." He did not take her offered hand so she widened her smile.

"As I said on the phone, I'm here to interview you about Dexter Hoyt for *Art World*."

"Come in."

He didn't offer to take her coat so she kept it on and followed him into a large, sparsely furnished room where she stopped dead and gasped.

Luminous against stark-white walls, Dexter Hoyt's paintings glowed like jewels—no other word was adequate. Heart beating in her ears, she counted them. *Thirteen.*

"I had no idea—"

"Few people have."

"Your collection is going to send my article over the top."

"How so?"

She turned from the paintings in surprise. Lean and sinewy, with short-clipped light-brown hair and a spare, closed face, Quick returned her gaze coolly.

"Because, Professor, if none of these Hoyts has been reproduced, they are going to make a terrific splash in *Art World*."

"I don't think so."

"Sorry?"

"I don't allow anyone to photograph my paintings."

My paintings!

"But why not? Naturally, I don't mean all of them, just three or four. Hoyt himself is giving me permission to publish photos of his art with my article." She didn't blush at her lie.

"Then photograph what Dex has on hand in his studio. Though," he said with a small smile, "I don't think it's much. He hasn't been working well lately."

Suddenly she felt an urgent need to rescue something from this meeting.

"You do know that the more attention your collection gets the more its value rises?"

"Happily I don't plan to retire on Matilda Roth Hamilton's article."

She wanted to slice his shins. Instead she said with what she hoped was deep sarcasm, "May I then at least have your oh-so-valuable assessment of Hoyt's work? Otherwise why bother to give me an interview at all?"

He motioned her to a low chair, took a seat on a white bench opposite her and leaned forward, wrapping his arms around sharp knees. "*Art World* warned me about you. What do you want to know?"

She produced her notebook, clicked her pen.

"Background, first. I know you're a professor at Madison, right?"

"Nuclear physics, yes. I don't teach, you understand, I run a lab. As a research scientist I've brought in millions in grant money for the University."

"Ultra impressive. And you're a Wisconsin native?"

"Illinois-born."

"Married? Children?"

"What possible relevance can my marital status have?"

She cast about wildly. "Perhaps if your wife didn't support your collecting—"

"Let's address the topic at hand."

"Fine." She felt like a battlefield strewn with wounded. "Do you collect other artists as well?"

"Certainly. I must give you a tour some day."

"Those others, are they—"

He stood up in one fluid athletic motion. Clearly he felt the interview was going nowhere. "Naming 'other artists' in your article, Matilda, can hardy help Dex." He looked suggestively toward the door.

Maddening, maddening man! She dug in.

"Just a few more questions, please, Professor. How long have you been collecting Hoyt?"

"Exactly ten years come April."

"*Why* do you collect him? This is major major."

"Obviously because I think he's good."

"Right, so do I. But relatively speaking, he's still pretty obscure. What brought him to your attention?"

He sighed and folded his arms as though about to deliver a lecture. (But no, he didn't teach.) "You've heard of John Wilde?"

At last she was sure of the pronunciation of this Wisconsin artist. Not *wild* as in Oscar, but *WILdee*.

"Of course."

"Hoyt was his student. As such, he couldn't be ignored, especially as Wilde himself believed in his talent. Got him into a gallery or two, dropped his name into strategic ears."

He moved toward the paintings and stopped in front of a smallish canvas. She saw that it was a fantasy of woman as butterfly floating serenely on orange and black-veined wings against a dove-grey sky. She also saw that it was the same woman Hoyt had painted in "Woman with Snake."

"If you *do* know Wilde, you can see him stamped all over this painting of Dex's." In the silence that followed, Tillie realized he was testing her.

"Well," she said, gathering her wits. "The palette's something you'd find in a Wilde."

He frowned. "Not that often."

"Often enough." Stand your ground, Tillie. "True, Wilde's more transparent. He paints phantoms behind shadows, so to speak."

"Yes."

19

"So I wouldn't call Wilde *stamped* on this painting. In fact I see more Botticelli than Wilde, I always have in Hoyt's work. But I do see that both Wilde and Hoyt believed that reality is illusion. They're both painting other worlds."

Quick didn't agree or disagree, but at least he was no longer nudging her toward the front door.

"To get back to the reason you're here," he said, crossing his arms and rocking back on his heels. "About ten years ago, as I said, I began to buy a Hoyt here and there, no big investment. Then I waited for his stock to soar. When it didn't, I started buying him in earnest. I trusted Wilde. Hoyt was cheap now, but he was going to be big."

"You're honest at least."

"You think collectors buy art as a charitable cause?"

"Of course not. But with Hoyt—you *liked* his work."

"I did." Adam Quick smiled for the first time. "I found his pseudo-medievalism combined with an arcane futurism both"—he paused—"intriguing and insane. Rather like nuclear physics. And his brushwork is, of course, phenomenal. Perhaps better than Wilde's."

Retrieving the notebook she'd forgotten on a chair now would be awkward. She'd have to remember every word and get it all down back at the Ferry Manse.

"I no longer collect Hoyt, you know."

She stared at him in dismay. "You don't? Why? Don't you believe in him any more?" She felt unreasonably let down, betrayed even.

He shrugged. "We had a disagreement. Artists and collectors should never meet face to face, let alone live in the same town. It's incestuous, somehow. Look, Matilda, fascinating as this interview has been, I really can't tell you any more at this point."

Won't, she fumed silently. She zipped her briefcase shut ostentatiously, hoping the gesture might disarm him into saying something off the record. Her disappointment was deep. Hoyt and Quick were main sources for her article. Naively, she'd imagined both artist and collector being grateful for a national magazine's attention.

20

Quick held open his front door; she felt the cold.

"One thing more, Professor Quick. Can you at least say something about the subject of three of your Hoyts? I mean the butterfly woman and the small painting of a woman holding a lily—oh, and the blond madonna in a turban kissing a parrot. Obviously he used the same model over and over. She must have been extremely important to him."

Quick's face shut down altogether.

She pressed on. "Dexter told me that she's his neighbor—or was?"

She thought Adam Quick wasn't going to answer. Then he said:

"Liz Barker is her name. She used to be Liz Quick. Before she walked out on me."

CHAPTER SIX

Enveloped in ankle-length mink, Eleanora Klein dragged on a cigarette while her dog researched the perfect snowbank in which to pee. About Gigi Nora felt considerable guilt. Walking her last January, she'd slipped on black ice. Six weeks to recover from concussion—if, she told herself bleakly, she ever had. Now every day she woke swearing she'd walk Gigi and every day she found a dozen excuses not to. She was a damn coward.

A red Ford truck, chains spitting snow, swerved into the exclusive drive that accessed Nora Klein's lake property. The ruddy-faced, silver-haired driver waved, killed the motor and jumped out.

"Morning, beautiful."

"Are you addressing me or Gigi?"

Gigi at least was in the truck driver's arms, nuzzling his pockets for the treats he always carried. Barker popped a Charlie Bear into her mouth and dropped her gently into a snowbank where she ecstatically writhed and rolled.

"You, Mrs. Klein. Who else?"

"Any number of women, I'm sure."

"Rot and rubbish, you know there's never been anyone but you. Except, of course, my inimitable blond wildcat—" Face suddenly crumpling, he buried his face in his unintentionally comic yellow Farm and Fleet gloves.

"Smitty, *don't*."

"Why the hell can't I get a grip on myself!"

"You're pushing it too hard, dear friend." She spun her cigarette into a snowbank; linked her arm through his. "For gods sake, give yourself time to heal. I know of what I say." She piloted him toward her brick front-door walk that had been swept exquisitely clean at six a.m. by her yard man.

"Coffee's on," she said briskly. "And I desperately need help with 17 down. What's a word for *stubborn,* twelve letters? Also I know you want to know how *I'm* doing, right? All shall be revealed over a cup—"

"Excuse me!"

They stopped and stared. A young woman was advancing down the private drive, a briefcase slung over her shoulder. She was sheathed in long black coat with a fox-fur collar. Her thick, unruly red hair was barely disciplined by a pair of huge grey rabbit-fur ear-muffs.

Nora dropped Smitty's arm, yanked her mink close. "What the hell's *she* selling?" she hissed.

"Sorry to interrupt." The young woman smiled, looking expectantly from one blank face to the other. "I'm gathering background material for my article. You know: the town he lives in, the lake he swims in, the neighborhood he walks in. I was following the lake road until— bang—it ended right here at this drive."

"Indeed it does end," said Nora frigidly. "This is m*y* drive."

"But is that fair?"

"I don't understand you."

"Well, people should be allowed to go on, shouldn't they?"

At a loss, Nora turned to Smitty, then quickly away when she saw the smile that lit his homely, kind face. It was the first smile she'd seen since his wife's disappearance and ghastly reappearance in the Henge. She, Nora, had been waiting to receive that smile for many weeks. But this smile was not for her.

Her companion in the black and red lumberjack shirt dove in.

"Smitty Barker, local vet. And this is my old friend Eleanora Klein. Now, Red, you sure aren't from Mills Lake, are you?"

"From New York." She offered her hand. "Matilda Roth Hamilton."

Smitty grasped hers and pumped it. "Pleased to meet you Ms. Hamilton. You're a ways from home."

"A big ways."

"Nora, this young lady looks like she could do with a cup of hot coffee." He nudged Nora, who had not said a word.

"Do join us, Ms. Hamilton," Nora said formally.

Inside, they piled their wraps on an antique chest in the hall, Gigi sniffing Tillie's boots and growling low in her throat. "It's okay, Gigi," said Nora. Guided by the perfume of fresh-perking hazelnut coffee, they filed through the kitchen into a sunny breakfast room.

Impulsively Tillie turned to her hostess. "Oh, how perfectly *perfect*! If you could *see* my broom closet of an apartment! The space, the light you've got! And those plates on the walls—" She felt as though she were babbling—how humiliating—at the same time realizing that she'd stumbled into the kind of house she'd always dreamed of. "Quimper, aren't they?"

"If you ever have the privilege of examining my house, Ms. Hamilton, you'll discover that France is my country of choice."

"Call me Tillie," she said, undaunted. She raised her eyes to the ceiling, from which hung a chandelier so delicately carved out of what she guessed was ash wood that it seemed to float in space. "Oh, Nora—may I call you that? How stunning!"

Nora frowned. She knew the chandelier was stunning: every room in her house and every thing in those rooms was stunning. She lifted the coffee pot in what Tillie interpreted as a let's-get-this-over-gesture, while Smitty made a gallant show of seating Tillie—as though it's *his* damn breakfast room, seethed Nora. She forced a smile and offered a plate.

"Sticky buns. I don't bake, as Smitty knows, but Waterhouse does it for me oh so well."

Tillie and Smitty fell upon the buns while Gigi danced around the table, alert for treats.

"Don't dare feed her, Smitty," warned Nora, looking at Tillie.

"But she's totally adorable!" cried Tillie.

"And knows it." Nora lit another cigarette.

Tillie looked into the little dog's fathomless eyes. "Oh, may I walk her while I'm here, Nora?" she said impulsively. "I'd love to."

"Surely you're too busy exploring the town he lives in, the lake he swims in, the bars he drinks in—"

Tillie decided to ignore the sarcasm. "That hardly takes up my whole day. Mr. Hoyt sleeps rather late, so early mornings I've nothing particular to do."

Nora actually smiled. "Well, if you *must* walk my dog, early morning's the best time. But back to your mission. I'm interested. Who in Mills Lake can possibly have background worth gathering?"

"I should have explained. I'm here for *Art World*, the prestige magazine?" She glanced around the table expectantly but met only blank incomprehension. "My editor assigned me an in-depth article on Dexter Hoyt. We both think he's a coming artist." She saw Nora and Smitty exchange glances she couldn't translate. "You must know him. He lives only blocks away, up on Coolidge Street."

Smitty finally broke the silence. "Sure we know him, Matilda. Most people do, I imagine. Actually he lives in the old carriage house right back of me that once belonged to the Ferry property. Thing is, he's kind of reclusive, doesn't even talk to his own sister. If you're looking for folks who know him, I can't think of anybody who's real close. Can you, Nora?"

Nora touched his rough paw with an iridescent fingernail. "Liz must have known him, Smitty," she murmured. "Didn't he paint her?"

"Liz," he said, and swallowed. He turned to Tillie. "Sure, my Liz knew who Dexter Hoyt was, she even knew he painted her. But she never posed for him or anything. It was strictly a one-way—"

"—Infatuation?"

"You got it, Matilda. I doubt they ever exchanged ten words. But, believe me, Liz was totally aware he was watching her. She used to say she could feel his eyes sucking the soul out of her. It gave her the creeps, to the point where one day I went over and banged on Hoyt's door. When he opened it I asked him point-blank what the hell he was doing freaking out my wife. I mean, sometimes she sunbathed nude in our garden, for chrissake! As was her right to do."

"And what happened, Doctor Barker?"

At her use of his professional title, Smitty melted. "As I said, I stormed Hoyt's dump of a studio, but he was, how should I say it, very welcoming. I hadn't expected that. And he showed me some of his stuff and in my humble opinion it was damn good."

"Of course it was," smiled Tillie, heart soaring.

"And sure, Liz was in a couple of paintings. But so, so—" He spread large and callused but surprisingly sensitive hands.

"Transformed?" said Tillie.

"That's the word I'm after, thanks. I mean it was Liz but it *wasn't* Liz, if you get me."

"I do. To me, Hoyt's paintings aren't about people at all but about innocence—or, conversely, the most subtle corruption." She turned politely to Nora to include her in the conversation and for the first time really registered her. Nora's dark brown hair was perfectly styled to cup her small head like the calix of a flower. Her eyes were lake-ice grey. She might be forty or sixty; she seemed curiously ageless. The word "refined" leapt into Tillie's mind. Yes. Eleanora Klein was refined.

Tillie remembered they were talking about Hoyt. "Of course you're familiar with his paintings, Nora."

"Not at all."

"Really!"

"Why should I be? I'm a psychiatrist, which is to say a scientist. Art has little significance to me."

"May I say I think it should have? Dexter Hoyt's paintings are a virtual psychology textbook. 'Woman with Snake' is a prime example, but every one of his canvases intrigues me psychologically. One in particular."

The retired psychiatrist rolled her eyes and snapped a silver lighter at another cigarette tip.

"The painting I'm talking about is dark—literally and figuratively—and in his best what I call abstract-magic style. You look at it and it's a boat. But then it isn't, it's an insect. When I asked what kind of insect—if that's what it is—Hoyt shrugged and said it was whatever the viewer saw. But then, imposed over the beetle—if it *is* a beetle—is a third abstraction—"

"Obviously a fatally cluttered painting," said Nora dismissively. As she ground out her cigarette Tillie noticed she wore

26

no rings. So not married, perhaps never was? "Don't you agree, Smitty?"

"I don't know what the hell you're talking about, Nora. *And* Tillie."

"But it's *not* cluttered." Tillie forged on. "It's a meticulously painted work of abstract art."

"So what is this 'third abstraction'?" Nora grimaced at her friend. "I suppose dear Liz, as usual."

"Oh, please." Smitty turned away, pained.

"I'm not sure, but something white: a sweater or scarf, a rug. For all I know, maybe it's the moon."

They looked at her blankly.

"But I'm curious about something else that maybe you can help me with. I've only been here a day and a half and already quite a few people have mentioned somebody named Liz. Mr. Hoyt, for one, now both of you. Another person who mentioned her is someone who collects his work."

Smitty's face darkened. He clamped both hands on the table and shoved back his chair. "Would that be Adam Quick?"

"Yes, that's the man I interviewed."

"Bastard!"

Tillie's delicate brows climbed her forehead.

"Pardon my French, that's strictly off-record. I've nothing against Quick."

"The hell you haven't!" Nora stabbed out her fourth cigarette and jumped up to clear the table.

The veterinarian leaned across the table. "No way you'd know this, Matilda, but before we married, Liz Barker was Liz Quick. And she had a whole bunch of damn good reasons for leaving Adam. *That's* what I've got against him."

Nora turned, plates in her hands. "I'd like to put this on record. For some reason Quick blames *me* for her leaving him when I had nothing remotely to do with it.

"Why would Professor Quick blame *you*?" Tillie, alert and curious.

"Maybe because at one of the neighborhood social events—
they can be dreary as hell sometimes—I did a bit of psychoanalyzing
of Quick. Liz was there and listening. She left him soon after. I'm
sure what I said had nothing to do with that. She simply decided she
preferred a gentleman over a tyrant. We all know everybody loves
the local vet." She was smiling, but her voice had a bitter edge.

"May we go back to Hoyt," Tillie coaxed, pretending igno-
rance of the undercurrents swirling about. "After all, he's the reason
I came all the way from New York. Dr. Barker says he's reclusive.
Does that mean I won't find anybody who'll talk to me about him?"

Smitty rubbed his jaw, reflecting. "Oh, I'd guess the whole
town has *something* to say about Dex, right, Nora?"

But Nora was clearing the table and all business. "May I remind you, Smitty, that you have an 8:30 appointment with Gigi and
that all three of us are going to be late?"

"Right-o," said Smitty. He rose, gestured Tillie to go before
him. As they filed to the front door, though, he stopped her with a
tap on her arm and leaned close to whisper.

"I recommend you talk to Wilk Steeves, our city manager.
That man's got a finger on a lot of pulses."

Tillie nodded her thanks and they caught up with Nora.

"So, Nora, is it all right if I come by for Gigi tomorrow about
eight?"

Nora smiled. "Be my guest."

CHAPTER SEVEN

Dark clouds looked eager to unload another three inches on the city as Tillie turned out of Nora Klein's cul-de-sac onto the road that ran along the east shore of Mills Lake. Instantly she realized that Gigi was not leash-trained; the unexpectedly powerful little dog tugged and pranced, casting reproachful "hurry up" looks over her shoulder.

Obviously Saturday morning in Mills Lake was prime dog walking time. They passed a German shepherd, a handsome tri-color collie, a golden, a beagle named Georgia, and a huge, hairy, muzzled dog she couldn't identify. Lusting to take on the big boys, Gigi jerked her along. By the time she braked to explore a hydrant, Tillie was nursing her shoulder. Suddenly Gigi flattened her ears and bared her teeth. With a snarl and a rush a big black dog burst upon them with the seeming goal of swallowing Gigi for breakfast. Volleys of insane barking.

"Please control your dog!"

"Fletcher, off! I'm so sorry!"

"You should be!" gasped Tillie.

The big German shepherd under control, the man leaned down to caress Gigi's ears; she leaned into his hand, whimpering with pleasure. "Please tell the lady, Gigi, that it's *you*—not Fletch—who picks the fight every time."

"I don't believe it!"

"You don't know much about the fox terrier-chihuahua mix, do you? Little Napoleons, champion fight-pickers of the dog world."

No wonder Nora didn't walk her own dog.

"I'm Wilk, by the way. Wilk Steeves."

She extricated her hand from Gigi's leash. "Matilda Roth Hamilton."

"Pleased to meet you, Matilda. Are you new in town?"

"Extremely."

He stood up, wound Fletch's leash around his glove, touched the brim of his plaid wool cap and walked on. He'd put half a block between them before he turned around.

"Say, Matilda," he called. "A bunch of us meet at Waterhouse Bakery for coffee Saturday mornings after the dog run. Care to join us?"

Tillie was about to say no when she remembered Smitty Barker's "Wilk Steeves has his finger on the pulse of the town." So this must be the City Manager himself.

"Where is Waterhouse?"

Over his shoulder he shouted "Downtown on East Lake, you can't miss it. Save you a chair."

Two deep chairs and a table piled with magazines filled Waterhouse's front window. When she opened the door, clattering cups, hissing espresso machines and voices ricocheting off the walls assaulted her. She registered shelves stacked with jars of honey and syrups, breads and pastas; beyond these, a smiling, frizzy-haired woman stood behind a tiny counter fielding a line of customers six deep. Peering through the fog of coffee fumes, noise, and drying parkas, she saw that the dog-walking man was nowhere in sight.

"Care to join us?" A small woman smiled from her perch on a high chair. "It's packed in here and going to get worse. I'm Victoria and this is Maurice."

Tillie accepted the offered chair. "Thanks so much. I'm supposed to be meeting somebody"—she checked around again—"but I don't see him."

"There are tables in back," said Victoria, dividing a scone precisely in two and offering one half to Maurice. "Your friend might be there."

But he invited me," thought Tillie, *"so he should be waiting for me.*"

"If you want order, you'll have to join the line at the counter. Nobody waits on you here." Victoria again. Evidently Maurice was the strong silent type.

Suddenly Tillie felt very lonely perched on her high chair, a stranger surrounded by strangers, waiting for a stranger she'd met for two minutes walking a dog.

"I guess I can't wait after all." She pointed to the line now longer by three Mills Lakeians. "Thank you, Victoria and Maurice, for sharing your table." Victoria nodded and smiled; buried in his newspaper, Maurice didn't seem to register her leaving—as he hadn't her coming.

Outside she pulled her fox collar around her neck. Men! You couldn't trust 'em. Not never, not nohow.

Wondering how to fill the time until her appointment with Hoyt, she realized that the Manse was only blocks away across the Common where she'd seen the skaters that first morning in Mills Lake. Just yesterday, was it? So much had happened since.

"So goodbye to all that," she sighed and was almost across the park when she heard a shout. She hesitated, decided it could have nothing to do with her, marched on.

"Matilda Roth Hamilton, wait up!"

She turned to see a man waving a plaid cap. The City Manager. Should she ignore him, or slow down and let him catch up. She decided on the latter. Infuriatingly, when he did, his face was split by a grin.

"How come you didn't show?" he said, planting himself in front of her. "I'm not used to being stood up by New Yorkers." But he was laughing, eyes crinkling. Sky-blue eyes, Paul Newman eyes. Her eyes were dark as coffee.

Wanting to smile back, she instead arranged her features into a rebuke. "I did show. It's *you* who didn't."

"Look," he said, "I did save you a chair. But I guess I should've come up front to look for you."

"You should have. Why didn't you?"

"Frankly I didn't think there was a chance in a million you'd come."

"You doubted me," she said, thawing a bit.

"I did and I apologize. So you're staying at the Ferry?"

"Yes," wondering how he knew.

31

"Let me walk you there."

She'd expected him to invite her back to Waterhouse, so that when he put his hand under her elbow as they stood on the curb about to cross Madison Street, she slipped away from it, disappointed. They walked in silence past the bank and post office, crossed Mulberry Street heading for the black wrought-iron fence that signaled the Ferry Manse.

"Guess this is where I leave you. Are you comfortable at the Manse?"

"A tad too period for me, but yes."

"Maybe we can do coffee some other time."

Tillie frowned. "I don't think so, I'm only here a couple of days. You wouldn't know" (what city manager *would* know about art?) "but I'm here to do an article on a considerable but undiscovered artistic talent."

"You mean Dexter Hoyt, don't you. And the article's for a magazine called *Art World.* And you've already talked to Adam Quick, Smitty Barker, Nora Klein and Hoyt himself. *And* walked Nora's dog."

Tillie's eyes widened. "So it's true then, what Doctor Barker said!"

"And Doc libeled me how?"

"He said your finger is always on the pulse of the town."

He ducked his head modestly. "Well, that's my job, you know. Besides, never underestimate the power of a small town."

She knew she must connect with him.

"Mr. Steeves, obviously you know Mills Lake from top to bottom. I can't tell you how much I'd appreciate your giving me an interview for my article. For, you know, depth, background, local dynamics. Would that be possible?"

He frowned. "Actually, I don't think I'd be much use to you."

She hung her very pretty head.

He fished out what she saw was a pocket date book and flipped through it. "Though I see I do have an open window between ten-thirty and eleven Monday morning."

Tillie beamed. "Perfect. Thank you." With formality she shook his hand.

*****

The Municipal Building rose in brick splendor, the newest building in a town that had impressed Tillie as determined to preserve its nineteenth-century past. Tugging open the entrance door, she looked about for directions and spotted an open office door where a pretty, dark-haired woman sat behind a terminally cluttered desk in a room designated "Main Street Program."

"Excuse me," she said. "I have an appointment with the city manager?"

"Upstairs," said the woman, buried to her chin in what might be gift baskets for an upcoming raffle.

She jogged to the second floor and found a large open office with multiple cubicles behind a counter. "Hello?" she called out. From one cell a curly grey head popped up like bread from a toaster.

"Where can I find the city manager, please?"

"Do you have an appointment?"

"I do."

"Straight ahead," said the woman, "then a right. He's down the end of the corridor."

Ironic: the man with his finger on the public pulse hidden in the remotest reaches of the new building. Traversing that corridor and locating a door that read "W. Steeves, Cty Mgr," she knocked.

"Come in," said a voice she didn't recognize.

Steeves sat behind a desk so large it left no space for any thing else in the room except a wood visitor's chair. A huge pair of horned-rim glasses decorated his nose and he was eating a large sugar donut. As they stared at each other, she felt the magic of their Saturday encounter die a sudden and unlovely death.

"I remember now, we have an appointment." He licked his sugary fingers one by one and waved them in the air to dry. "You're looking for local background, right?"

"Right."

33

"For an article about Dexter Hoyt."

"Yes," she said, brightening. At least he remembered. She fished her tape recorder out of her briefcase. "Do you mind?"

"Actually, Matilda Roth Hamilton, I do. Very definitely I do not want to go on record about this."

Deflated, she stowed the recorder and pulled out her notebook.

"So shoot."

"First question, Mr. Steeves: how well do you know Dexter Hoyt?"

He tossed his head side to side, rubbed his jaw, frowned. "As well as most, I guess. I've seen a few of his paintings—pretty good, in my opinion. Traded small talk with him once or twice over a brew at Bill and Helen's. That's about it." He yanked off the horned-rims and massaged the bridge of his nose. She sensed him holding back.

"Nothing else?"

"Only if it's strictly off-record." He jabbed the horn rims at her to make sure she got the message. Today the blue eyes were cool as an April lake.

"It will be, of course."

"Okay. Sorry to say, Hoyt has a very bad habit of not paying his bills. Light and Water Department's leaned on me more than once to deliver the news that his electricity and heat would be cut off if he didn't pay. Not my favorite task, playing bill collector, but better than L & W shutting him down without notice in winter."

"And what happened? Did he pay the bills?"

"Don't ask me how, but eventually they always got paid."

By somebody, she thought, making a note, but by whom? and was about to ask when his phone jangled. He picked up, listened in silence. Finally: "Appreciate your including me, Chief. Eleven-thirty? I'll be there."

Tillie checked her watch; five minutes before he'd dismiss her. 'Chief' must be the Chief of Police? Suddenly she saw Dexter Hoyt's face clenched in bitterness, telling her that his muse Liz Barker had been found dead in ice and that the town believed he killed her.

Pretend to know what it's all about and maybe he'll tell me, decided Tillie.

"Sorry to cut this short."

"The Chief wants to see you about Liz Barker, doesn't he."

Steeves aimed his glasses at her. "*She*," he corrected. "And what do you know about that?"

"Quite a lot. The subject of my article is *involved*, to put it mildly. Hoyt tells me everybody in town thinks he killed her."

His eyebrows shot up. "Really? That's extreme. Maybe a few do, certainly not 'everybody.' But these are early days. Nobody even knows whether it was murder or not."

"Of course it was murder," said Tillie boldly. "Tragic but true: beautiful dead blonde equals murder victim."

He threw her a startled glance, then checked his watch.

"Sorry, I have to run," he said, rising and squeezing around the preposterously large desk. He threw her a distracted glance and was gone.

CHAPTER EIGHT

The Chief of Police massaged the bridge of her nose as she surveyed the room and decided to go with it.

"Well," said Maureen Sherpinski, carefully making eye contact with each of the thirteen people assembled. "It looks like murder after all."

An exhalation of something like satisfaction stirred the air.

"I never figured anything but." A small, wiry blond officer caressed the gun holster on her right hip.

"Good work, Moss. The rest of us—heck, I guess we were just waiting around for evidence." She bit her lip. She *must not* air her purely personal dislike of their newest officer in public. "Okay, everybody, the latest is in. Madison says they've found what might be traces of drugs in the victim's remains."

"What kind of drugs?"

Sherpinski acknowledged Sergeant Crosby, her personal favorite among the force, though she'd never admit it. "Identifying the drugs will take longer, John, so I'm told."

"Like what—a year?"

She stabbed a finger at him as though to say "Bingo!" and laughed. "Let's hope not."

"I don't know about the rest of us, Chief," said Crosby, "but while Madison fiddles around, I personally feel an urgent need for you to update the people in this room on *our* progress on this case."

Wilk Steeves found himself joining the murmur of agreement.

Sherpinski reached for a folder on her desk, extracted a pair of glasses from a breast pocket. "Okay, here goes the update. 'February second, 1980'"—

"Objection!" Captain Mark Witter, a veteran of the force, was on his feet. "This is top security information and there are people in this room who certainly aren't police."

"Noted," said Sherpinski, with her minimalist smile. "But surely, Captain, you of all officers know our mission statement by heart?"

Witter frowned.

"Then let me remind you. 'The task of keeping Mills Lake safe and free from crime will be implemented always *by partnering with the community.*' Who here today represent the community?"

Wilk looked around, raised his hand. "City Manager Steeves, here. And I see that our Chamber of Commerce president is present as well."

Witter grudgingly subsided and Sherpinski took over again.

"MLPD's main thrust has been to establish Elizabeth Barker's movements prior to February second. *When* was she murdered—as it now seems probable she was—and *why* wasn't she reported missing by her husband, Dr. Smith Barker? Above all, *if* Ms. Barker was murdered, who wanted her dead? The Jefferson County coroner estimates she went into the lake late in December, Madison seconds that. But back to the question of why her husband didn't report her missing."

There was a sitting up to attention.

"Actually the answer's pretty simple"— Sherpinski enjoying her inside information. "For years Liz Barker's flown down to Fort Myers, Florida, to visit her sister Cynthia Easton in December. Doc Barker confirms this ritual was set in cement. He also complains, by the way, that Liz timed her visit to get out of buying him a Christmas present.

Officer Moss hooted.

Sherpinski saw she had everyone's attention. "But this December Liz failed to show up in Fort Myers."

Wilk Steeves raised his hand like a schoolboy. "You sure the sister was definitely expecting her?"

"According to Dr. Barker, yes."

"Then why didn't the sister sound the alarm?"

"I'd like Crosby to speak to that."

Crosby got to his feet. He was a stocky, almost-handsome man with buzz-cut hair and a sincere frown that bisected his forehead. Always modest, he tried to downplay his unswerving determination to be the best MLPD sergeant on record.

"Three days after the victim was taken from the water—uh, *ice*—the Chief sent me to Florida to find the sister. I did find her, living in a pretty swell condo on the water. After I asked a bunch of routine questions, Mrs. Easton rummaged in a desk and handed me a letter. Upon examination, I saw that it was from her sister Elizabeth Barker, dated November twenty-first, 1979." He reached for his notes and his glasses, positioned them on his nose. "In it Ms. Barker wrote—and I quote: 'So sorry for canceling, Cyn, but for personal reasons, I need some alone time this year. Call you soon, darling.'"

Sherpinski shot out of her chair, planting knuckles on her desk, looming over the assembly like a fierce bird of prey.

"Let's run with this—Witter, Moss, Selck. If Liz didn't show up at her sister's in Fort Meyers last December, where was she?"

"In the lake." Chamber president Alysia Ford spoke for the first time and looked surprised that she had. She looked around for affirmation. "*Liz Barker was already in the lake, right?*"

Again Captain Witter jumped to his feet. "Then what's this bullshit about canceling her sister because she needed time alone?"

"Exactly that, Captain—bullshit."

"You're saying what, Ms. C of C?"

"I know I don't have any business butting in, but this is a public forum, right?" She appealed to Sherpinski, who nodded. "Okay, what I'm saying is: I don't believe Liz Smith wrote that letter to her sister, I think it was forged. Don't ask me who forged it. But whoever did—I say that's our murderer."

CHAPTER NINE

Three more days to accomplish a miracle.

Tillie had begun wearing clothes she'd worn the day before. Her plan, conceived in far-away New York, had been to conquer Mills Lake rapidly and then—as the success and fame of her project grew—to emerge as the ultimate New York professional, shrouded in cosmopolitan mystique. And when she'd discovered that the Opera House was also a bistro where a couple named Jason and Beth Dunn were making culinary news, she imagined throwing a party for the whole Mills Lake "cast"— charging the shebang to *Art World*, of course. The more she thought about it, the more she felt that *Art World* owed her.

Except that interviews with Dexter Hoyt were going so badly that she was seriously beginning to wonder whether she'd wind up with an article at all. Though he'd stopped offering her his dreadful tea (was it really tea?) he'd withdrawn emotionally into some kind of holding cell from which he was emitting only the weakest of signals. Worse, he'd stopped sharing insights into his art. And his insights were to be the gist of her article.

Today she was going to fight back, zeroing in on a painting she planned to make the centerpiece of her article. "Woman with Snake" was simple in execution: a fair (again) woman glowing like a pearl against a densely nuanced dark background. But she didn't think Hoyt's "message" was simple at all. From a mound of emerald turf at the woman's feet, a snake spiraled upward, its flickering tongue almost penetrating the woman's pudenda. *Almost* was the key. If this isn't about frustrated male desire, thought Tillie, fire me as an art critic.

She knocked a fifth time.

"Entrez!" Hoyt threw open the door.

As she stepped inside he lunged at her, pinning her to the wall.

"*What are you doing!*" She panicked, twisting her head away from his hot breath. Ducking, squirming and shoving, she managed to work herself free of him and stood there shocked and panting.

Hoyt's hair was rumpled, his chin dark with stubble. He grinned at her and made a sweeping bow.

Good god, he's drunk, realized Tillie.

"Nice cup o' tea, love?" he said in a terrible attempt at a British accent.

"No, thank you." Her voice shook.

"Funny, in' it, how people always call a cup of tea a *nice* cup but nobody ever offers you a *nice* cup of coffee. Why's that?" He staggered and grabbed for a chair. "Actually, Matilda, I am in possession of the answer, and the answer is that coffee tastes good and tea tastes like such shit they've got to peddle it as "nice." So no tea, though it's my shitty potion of choice and you should be drinking it if only to please *me*. Then how may I serve my beautiful biographer today?"

Should she ignore his condition and press on with the interview—or exit pronto by the front door.

She couldn't leave, the days left were too precious. She decided to humor him.

"You can serve me, Mr. Hoyt, by dropping the sulky genius bit and getting serious about this article."

She expected outrage; instead he grinned.

"But I *am* a genius and I *am* sulky."

"Then can you please get over it—not the genius, of course, but the sulky?" Yet by now she was laughing too.

"You really think I should? *I* don't, because then you won't find me half as fascinating." He lurched to the panel of north windows overlooking the Garden of Liz. He's obsessed with that view, thought Tillie, not for the first time. Outside the grey winter sky was thickening into early twilight.

"I promise I'll find you *more* fascinating, Mr. Hoyt. Look, I believe in you and I persuaded my editor to run with this story. But frankly—forgive me for saying this—*in New York you are nobody*. Nobody from the Hinterlands, as we call them, is anybody until they penetrate the New York consciousness. And you're going to stay that way unless you get some media buzz. Like this article of mine."

"'I'm Nobody,'" he mocked, pressing his hands to his chest like a nineteenth-century Emily Dickinson. "'Who are you? Are you Nobody, too?'" So he knew Dickinson's famous lines, perhaps read her. "*You* will be nobody if you don't get your unknown genius scoop. *Because, baby, I am about to explode* without you."

Tillie clutched her notebook protectively to her chest. What to make of this new, almost expansive Dexter Hoyt as opposed to the moody artist she'd been dealing with? Alcohol, yes; but not only alcohol, she decided. Had he finally got a big commission? A more well-healed patron than Adam Quick? That might explain his strange mood.

She leaned forward with an encouraging smile. "Tell me what's happened, please," she said. "Good news, I'm assuming."

"Goodest of the good." Hoyt grinned, throwing back another swallow of something amber in a dirty glass. He got up and ran-sacked papers, finally pulling out a brochure and thrusting it into her hand.

An irrational dread seized Tillie making the print swim before her eyes. Blinking hard, she brought it into focus.

> Dexter Hoyt is one of three coming artists that Art Institute of Chicago takes pride in showcasing at its annual "Welcome Genius" event. Save the date for a gala black-tie reception, launched by a welcome from Museum Director Bingham Taft White and capped by an appreciation by eminent Chicago art critic, Bethany Gibbs . . .

"Impressed, New York? I see you are. Eyes bugging out of your head."

Oh, god. Was Chicago going to recognize Hoyt before her article had a chance to appear? If the event took place *after,* she was home free: she would have scooped Chicago with a visionary article—almost genius itself. She forced herself to look at the "Welcome Genius" date.

May 5, 1980.

Art World hit stands the fifteenth of each month.

She took a deep breath and held out her hand.

"Congratulations, Mr. Hoyt, I couldn't be more thrilled for you."

"Not bad, is it."

"Not bad at all. But for now"—she was surprised at the courage it took even to mention *Art World*—may we please focus on *our* article? My time here is limited and I really want to go deeper into your work and life."

"Deep away," he slurred. Decidedly, he was getting drunker by the minute.

"Then let's talk, this time in depth, about 'Woman with Snake.'"

Hoyt tossed back his head to finish off his glass. "Not a favorite of mine."

"Not? I'm surprised, *I* think it may be your masterpiece. But even if you underrate it, I want to zero in here. Myself, I interpret 'Woman and Snake' as all about frustrated male desire."

"Frustrated male desire? You jest." He looked around for his bottle.

"More specifically about *your* desire." She got up, tripped over a stack of frames and sat down next to him on the sagging couch. "May I run with this, please? I'm referring to your desire for the woman out your rear window. The gardening woman, the sunbathing woman, the woman who's the subject of most of the paintings I've seen. The beautiful Liz."

"No kidding," he said and belched.

Tillie shut her eyes on the off-chance that when she opened them she would find herself in a book-lined library before a crackling fire interviewing a man with a British accent wearing an ascot and tweeds. She opened them to Dexter Hoyt.

"So in 'Woman with Snake' you located your muse in the Garden of Eden—"

"Who says Eden? Show me the apple."

"But without Adam," she said, ignoring him, "who wasn't very persuasive anyway, as I recall." *Adam*—Adam Quick? Would Hoyt ever include Liz's ex in a painting? "So it's only Liz and a beautiful—if you admire reptiles—phallic snake. Which I believe is the artist himself. You, Dexter Hoyt."

Hoyt had located his bottle of Early Times; now he poured the remains into his glass as he stabbed a paint-stained forefinger at her.

"Sorry, wrong number, Matilda. Bet you never saw that Barbara Stanwyck classic, did you, no of course you didn't. Write it down, you're taking notes, aren't you? Stick in your article that Dexter Hoyt is also a classic film buff. *The Big Sleep, The Third Man, Double Indemnity*—shit, nobody ever made better."

"Will do." She scribbled note; it would be an interesting angle. "But those are old black and whites, and you're in love with color."

"Not on film. Color films are vulgar."

How—antique, thought Tillie. "Back to 'Woman with Snake'—"

"Yes, back to it, Matilda child." He looked around for his bottle. "But, child, your take is too, too pathetically easy."

"Is it? I don't think so." She was, in fact, quite proud of her reading. "How else could a person interpret it!"

"Let me educate you on interpretation, starting with the buyers of paintings. First off, buyers don't *interpret* anything. They look at a painting. They like the colors. Or the old guy reminds them of Uncle Fred. Or they think the painting'll go real good with the new dining room wallpaper. Or the price is right.

"So this shit about '*what does it mean*' means zero to the folks who buy. It strictly has to do with art critics trying to show off their 'taste and knowledge'—that's you. And that taste and knowledge depends on who's paying the critic to have it." He fell back against the couch pillows and squinted, trying to bring her into

43

focus. "Jesus," he said. "There's an outside possibility I may be drunk."

Oh, he was drunk alright, disgustingly drunk, and Tillie saw her beautifully constructed castle tumbling into ruins. She had no ammunition against inebriation.

"Mr. Hoyt," she said, trying to keep desperation out of her voice. "Please give me *something* about 'Woman with Snake,' can't you?"

"I'm trying." He struggled, trying to right himself, fell back. "But your male desire take's way off."

"I don't think so."

"Then think again. Think lesbian."

"*Lesbian?*"

"Ask yourself: What lesbian wouldn't love a snake's tongue licking her pussy."

Hoyt had passed out on the sofa and begun to snore. Not an obnoxious snore, Tillie noted: a gentle, whuffling snore like a tired dragon's. She found a heavy black pea coat and tucked it around him. Tearing a page from her notebook, she printed in urgent capitals: "Photographer Nathan Ely: appointment with you tomorrow at 10 a.m." and propped it against the empty bottle. Then she let herself out and started her hike back to the Manse.

Wind off the lake so bitter she could taste it; sizzling snow fast-carpeting shoveled walks. Definitely her designer coat was no match for Wisconsin winters. She'd bought it on sale after *Art World* hired her, a mad impulse that had taken her a year to pay off. At the same time she was glad of the cold. She needed to think and there was nothing like ten above zero snow to snap you to attention.

It was past five and dark as she walked down Coolidge. Cars were pulling into drives as people arrived home from work. Passing the three churches that marked the entrance of Coolidge, she turned right and headed downtown, the Mobile station at the corner of Main and Madison a garish beacon. Waving thanks to a car that hadn't tried to run her down, she crossed Main. You know it's a small town, she thought, when the major intersection's marked by a four-way stop.

Crunching down Madison—not everyone shoveled their sidewalks—she came to the library, a Gothic stone building she'd fallen in love with the first time she'd seen it. It was still open, warm light from tall windows beckoning patrons. *What every town in America needs is a Ferry library,* she thought; then on impulse she climbed two sets of shoveled steps and tugged open a heavy oak door.

To her right a fireplace surrounded by chairs, racks of magazines and new arrival books. Straight ahead the library check-out desk looking like every library check-out desk she'd ever seen. Heaven. Even her boots, softly sucking the linoleum, was a sound from childhood.

"Where can I find the reference section?" she asked the woman behind the counter, a petite lady with a friendly smile. Following her directions, she located a row of encyclopedias, pulled out the B-C volume, and opened her notebook. Under beetles" she finally zeroed in on the Deathwatch.

> To attract mates, these wood borers create a tapping or ticking sound that can be heard in the rafters of old buildings on quiet summer nights. They are therefore associated with quiet, sleepless nights and are named for the vigil (watch) kept beside the dying or dead, and by extension the superstitious have seen the deathwatch beetle as an omen of impending death.

Closing her notebook, Tillie reshelved the volume, nodded her thanks to the librarian behind the desk.

Across the street, stationed around the perimeter of the Common, tall retro lamps crowned with white globes illuminated snow-crusted benches and a deserted skating rink among the trees. She could make out the bandstand, dim as a ship at sea with snow drifts like white-caps curling its foundations. Across the park a Sentry grocery story and Timber Creek were still inviting customers, though she saw no pedestrians on the streets. And why would there be? Mills Lake was a shut-down early town, she'd decided, its citizens eager to retreat to their smug—surely she meant snug—middle-class comforts.

Yet Timber Creek reminded her she'd been doing pizza take-outs every evening and that her stomach had started to rebel. Should she dodge across the Common for a ham roll from Sentry's deli? She stepped off the curb, then remembered she'd stowed most of a BLT in the Manse refrigerator. Boycks was generous with the kitchen.

But forget supper, what about her article! How could she pull "Genius Discovered" out of the fire? Somehow she'd have to ditch the "unknown" angle. A painter feted by the Chicago Art Museum is no longer "unknown." Or her discovery.

She rounded the bank corner and, ducking her head against a cruel north wind, started up Mulberry. A few bitter stars gleamed like glass shards in the night sky. Her gloved fingers clutching the briefcase strap had gone quite numb, yet ahead shone the cheerful windows of the Manse. How wonderful to climb the great staircase, let herself into her room, make herself a cup of cocoa, and crawl with it into a flannel-sheeted bed.

And then—as calmly as possible—reassess her day.

It was then, so close to the glow of home and safety, that she forced herself to focus on what had been nagging her ever since leaving Hoyt's carriage house. And then again after she'd left the library.

She'd seen nobody, she'd heard nothing. Though on second thought, perhaps she had? A shadow thrown across the snow. A scrape of footsteps behind her—

By now she felt certain somebody was following her.

CHAPTER TEN

Bursting through the Manse door, she stumbled into the hall. What was *wrong* with her! All because of a feeling—nothing more—that she was being followed. Why hadn't she stopped and looked around to make sure? Stood her ground and confronted whoever was tracking her? So easy, though, for a stalker to vanish behind a tree trunk, slip into a shadow. And, she admitted, she was afraid to know.

"Join us, Tillie."

In the parlor Barry Boycks sat in front of a fire with two strangers. (Strangers, of course; she knew hardly anyone in town.)

"You look like you could use a cup of cheer."

"I could, actually. "

Boycks patted the cushion beside him, but first she went to the fireplace and stretched her hands to the blaze that smelled of pine and a wood she remembered from her childhood, hickory, maybe, from the stove in her grandparents' kitchen. Then she sat down and smiled tentatively at the couple opposite. Nobody spoke.

"Thanks, Barry," she said into silence, "it's been a long day."

The man had blond hair, startling black eyebrows, long legs that extended well beneath the coffee table that separated them. A white turtle-neck masked his jaw; a big signet ring on his right hand glinted as he lifted his glass. His wife (girlfriend?) was a petit woman with short-bobbed silver hair that argued with her youthful face and playfully tilted nose.

"Any day with Dexter would be a long day," said Barry. "Old Fashioned, darling, or dry martini, per Sue Ellen and Ted?"

Since he hadn't introduced her, she knew they'd been talking about her before she arrived.

"Old Fashioned, I guess."

Boycks juggled ice bucket and bottles, handed her a glass. She took a sip, seltzer tickling her nose. Her first Old Fashioned. "Excellent, Barry. Thank you."

Jabbing at his martini, Ted fished up an olive. "But do New Yorkers really *know* anything about the famous Wisconsin brandy Old Fashioned you're drinking?"

Tillie arrowed him a look over her glass. Obviously he'd had a drink or two—first Hoyt, now this Ted person.

"Oh, yes. Harry's on Sixth and Broadway makes an Old Fashioned to die for. *If,* that is, Harry allows Midwest yokels through the door." She stopped, appalled at what she'd made up on the spot, but not completely.

"So how's the article going?" Barry loudly overriding the silence that followed Tillie's little explosion. "Tillie's doing an important piece on Dexter Hoyt for some magazine—remind me of the name."

"*Art World.*"

He shrugged. "Myself, I've never heard of it, but us yokels are eagah and willin' to learn."

Barry Boycks had been so civil when she'd arrived, but his *yokels* cemented the "us against you" attitude Tillie's antennae had picked up the moment she'd walked into the room. She was about to reach for her briefcase and say good bye when her reporter's instinct clicked in. Suddenly she felt sure she could learn something valuable from this little cocktail party in front of the fire.

She held her half-empty glass out to Barry. "Seconds, bartender?"

"Even thirds, madam, just say the word. The same?"

"Please." She wouldn't drink any more, just pretend. Leaning forward she smiled at the couple opposite. Sue Ellen had not yet said a word. She noted that she too wasn't wearing a wedding ring.

"As Barry said, I'm doing an article on Dexter Hoyt for *Art World.* Do either of you know him?"

A look flew between Ted and Sue Ellen, then Ted threw back his head and swallowed the rest of his martini. "Oh, everybody knows Dex." He set down his glass. "*To their sorrow.*"

"*To their sorrow?*" Tillie was shocked. "What do you mean?"

"What do I mean, Sue Ellen? You tell her." It was a challenge.

Sue Ellen stared into her glass as though searching for an answer or perhaps deciding whether to speak at all.

"Ted and Dex have their differences," she said slowly. "A lot of people do, don't they, when they're neighbors? Dex doesn't live far from us. I know him because I'm an art teacher, Middle school, nothing professional—"

Ted sat up with such force that Sue Ellen had to steady her drink on the table. "Of course you're a professional, dammit. Why must you constantly underrate yourself!"

Turning from him, Sue Ellen threw Tillie a look. "So yes," she said, ignoring Ted's outburst, "I do know Dexter. Though, for your article, I can't stress this enough: he's a real artist and—whatever Ted says—I'm definitely not. Those who can do, you know; those who can't—"

"Teach?"

She nodded at Tillie, who thought she caught the silent message: *I have something I want to tell you, but not here and not now.*

"If we could talk tomorrow?" said Tillie.

Ted interrupted. "My wife's booked solid. I keep the house calendar so I know."

"Speaking of Dex." Boycks rose to warm his backside at the fire and the tension suddenly broke. "Did you know, Tillie, that our local vet has some of his paintings?"

"Only some?" said Tillie boldly. "As far as I can see, Doctor Barker's wife was Dexter Hoyt's obsession."

She was pleased to register alarm on three startled faces. What did *that* mean? She set down her glass and rose to go. "Good to meet you, Ted and Sue Ellen—I didn't catch your last name? "

"Gage," said Barry. "Ted and Sue Ellen Gage."

Tillie shouldered her briefcase. "I really have to look over my notes"—she turned and smiled at Boycks—"while I'm sober enough to read them."

*****

49

Upstairs she brushed her teeth, made a pass at her face, climbed into the four-poster and curled up knees to chin, a comfort position from childhood. Following her yoga method for relaxation, she took four deep breaths, held for a count of eight, released to the count of six. But this usually magic combination failed her. Fifteen minutes later she threw off the quilt, slid off the bed and slipped into her robe. She opened her briefcase, fished out the few notes she'd made about 'Woman with Snake,' sat down to read them— and stared at them in disbelief. At the time, she'd been sure she'd found the key to the universe; now she saw she only had Hoyt's denial that she understood the painting at all.

She tossed aside her notes and threw herself into the deep armchair in front of the fireplace.

Had Hoyt been saying Liz Barker was a lesbian? It seemed obvious he had; yet everything she knew about the dead woman contradicted that label. Married to Adam Quick who, under a bitter exterior, obviously still carried a torch for his former wife. Married to Smitty Barker who wept at the mention of her name. Seductive siren of Hoyt's paintings. . . .

So she'd been wrong. Then who or what was the snake? Or had Hoyt simply been baiting her? How likely.

Her eyelids fluttered; she realized she was exhausted. Remember, Tillie, she whispered, "Woman with Snake" is a vision, *not* a portrait." Her chin dropped to her chest, she whuffed a small snore. Poised on the brink of a deep dive into sleep, however, she sat up with a jerk.

Out there in the snowy dark. *Had* she been followed? If so, by whom and for what reason?

Adam Quick flashed across her mind. Beneath his coldness, she'd felt a reined-in interest in her. Had he loosed those reins, seen her leave the carriage house, decided to discover her destination?

She yawned wide. "Let it go for now," she told herself, folding her robe about her. "All will be solved." Yet her mind leapt to

Ted and Sue Ellen Gage: they bothered her. Spider Boycks had invited Tillie-fly into his parlor. Why? What was the subtext of that supposedly social encounter? She ticked off on her fingers:

You don't belong here.

Stay away from what doesn't concern you.

Sue Ellen may have something to tell you.

Dexter Hoyt is not liked in this town.

CHAPTER ELEVEN

"So, Crosby, what have you got?"

Sergeant Crosby leaned forward and handed her the notes he'd made on his trip to Florida to interview Liz Barker's sister, Cynthia Easton.

She rocked back, swivel chair squawking. He watched her eyes devour his report. Nothing like her, he thought, for nailing essentials at a glance.

"So we need a hand-writing expert."

"Yes."

"Madison again."

"Sure, Chief. But I got a thought. There's a local woman who analyzes handwriting as a kind of business on the side."

"How would that hold up in court?"

"Not well, probably. But how about she gives us a jump start and then we go to Madison?"

Crosby's strength was that he believed the MLPD could handle any situation. His weakness was the same.

"Who is she?"

"A Marianne Price, lives in one of the new condos out by the fish hatchery, gives talks around the area on handwriting analysis. I'm just saying we could try her before we call Madison. Pays to have different views."

Sherpinski studied him and sighed. She always leaned toward trusting Crosby.

"Okay, let this Price person have a go. But she'll need letters from Liz Barker for comparison. How sure are we that we can get ahold of those?"

"Smitty Barker and I are old friends. Do I have permission to contact him about this?"

Shepinski's phone jangled. She picked up and shot Crosby a green light.

*****

So that when Tillie rang Smitty Barker's doorbell by appointment that day, she was surprised to see a uniformed policeman hovering in the background. Stamping her boots on a mat, she looked questioningly at the veterinarian.

"Come in, Matilda. Here, give me your coat. Don't worry about tracking in snow, it's good for the rugs. No, you're not interrupting, John's on his way out."

The officer tapped Barker's shoulder with a manila envelope. "To progress."

"To progress." Smitty shut the door after him and turned to Tillie with a smile. "Coffee? I just brewed fresh."

"Lovely," she lied, disliking everything about coffee: its aroma, its taste, its mystique." She pulled off her ear muffs and shook out her wild red curls.

"You said on the phone you'd like to see the Hoyt paintings I own."

"Most definitely I would, Dr. Barker."

"Gosh sakes, call me Smitty, everybody does." He led the way to a small, crowded kitchen, Tillie dutifully following and accepting a cup of the black magic from his hand. "Cream or sugar? No? Now I gotta ask, just out of curiosity: who told you I owned some of Dex's work?"

"Barry Boycks, actually. I'm staying at the Ferry Manse."

"Wise decision, they take good care of you there."

Do they? wondered Tillie, remembering the fireside cocktail hour.

"So Barry said—"

"I should contact you about your Hoyts. Though I understand that you only have one or two. But for a devout believer in Hoyt's talent like me, seeing even two paintings of his would be major-major."

Barker nodded. "This way," he said. "My office is on the second floor. Liz didn't want my vet stuff *or* my paintings in sight, especially the Hoyts. For some reason, she hated them. Me, I think they're damn good. Though what do I know."

Boots clattering, Tillie followed him up a wood staircase. At the top, breathing heavily, Barker gestured her down a short hall. Preceding him, she entered a room that struck her immediately as unusual for a veterinarian. Yes, there were the expected anatomy charts of every animal from cats to cows, but there were also half a dozen elegantly framed oils and two watercolors. One of the oils she recognized from her evening with Adam Quick as a John Wilde.

Then she forgot everything else and zeroed in on the Hoyts.

Liz Barker again, and again.

The first painting was a knock-off of Botticelli's "Birth of Venus." Liz Barker had a flatter belly than Botticelli's Venus and Hoyt had substituted for the titian hair of the original the blondest of blonde tresses. What really grabbed Tillie's eye, however, were the peripheral figures. Instead of Boticelli's angels and goddess, there was Adam Quick, a lightning rod in his fist, while opposite a kneeling Dexter Hoyt offered the newly-born Venus a cornucopia of fruits and flowers.

"Well!"

"My sentiments exactly," said Barker drily. "Maybe it's good art, I'm no judge, but you can see why I'm not keen on publicizing it."

"And this one?" She homed in to scrutinize the second Hoyt. "I love it!" she laughed over her shoulder.

"Definitely, I do not."

Seated on a chair, a naked, voluptuous Liz leaned forward to cuddle a dachshund. The dog reared on its hind legs, front paws kneading her thighs, wet nose debating whether to poke into her bulging breasts or her crotch.

"If this isn't sex—" Smitty's face, his whole body tense with distaste.

"Oh, it's sex, all right," said Tillie comfortlessly. "And Hoyt's the dachshund, don't you think?" Barker flamed red; she regretted her words the moment she spoke them.

"I don't know. But as a member of the profession, I do believe that a woman heals better than any veterinarian possibly can."

She shook her head, confused. "So you're saying this painting's about healing? I'm not sure I agree with that."

"Well, I *know* it, Matilda. Sex is the answer to all maladies. Are we through here?"

"Not nearly."

But Barker took her arm and firmly ushered her out the door. They clattered down the stairs; at the bottom he faced her, still flushed.

"I hear you got a photographer to illustrate this article of yours?"

"Yes, a local. Nathan Ely—"

"He's good. Nevertheless, I refuse to give him permission to reproduce *my* Hoyts in any shape or form."

First Adam Quick, now Smitty Barker! "But Smitty, you must!"

"I don't think so, Matilda. Why should I! To be humiliated down the ages if Dex becomes famous? As you're promising all over town he will."

Just as suddenly as it flared, his anger collapsed. He reached out and awkwardly, even tenderly, patted her arm.

"Look, Tillie, when we met at Nora's I liked you right off, I truly did. A little more than like, actually. But I tell you plain: my ego—and my love for Liz—are way too fragile for this kind of public exposure."

He looked into her dark, wet eyes and could not bear her disappointment.

"Look," he said, "Ted Gage has a few Hoyts. Why don't you talk to him."

CHAPTER TWELVE

Sergeant Crosby hovered over a machine spitting copies of Liz Barker's letters: the crucial one Cynthia Easton had turned over to him in Florida, the rest lent to the MLPD by Dr. Barker on Sherpinski's word they'd be returned. Crosby locked the originals in the office safe, signed in the key, and left the Municipal Building by the rear exit. Squinting at a low grey sky, he decided snow was in the picture sooner than later. He unlocked the unmarked sedan, fired the engine, sank the seat belt clasp and pulled out of the lot heading for the new condos that lined the west bank of the state fish hatchery. It was a neighborhood unfamiliar to him in that, personally, he knew no one who lived there.

Turning into a cul-de-sac, he pulled up in front of a poker hand of five new structures, each sitting on its half-acre of snowy lawn that had been professionally landscaped with young birch and firs. Parking the squad, he walked up a sidewalk so immaculate it looked vacuumed and pressed an illuminated doorbell. Marianne Price opened the door.

She was a tall middle-aged woman swathed in a startlingly bright red sweater that fell below her knees. She'd twisted up her heavy black hair into a knot; huge hoops swung from her ears like chandeliers. Gold? If so, this was even more definitely not Crosby's world.

"Sergeant Crosby? Come in."

"Yes, ma'am." She struck him as a "ma'am" kind of woman.

He followed her down a hallway smelling of furniture wax until she halted on the threshold of—how else to describe it—a stage set. Surveying it, he felt he might drown before he could wade across the thick white carpet to the chair she indicated. Low white tables punctuated the expanse, every surface (he noted) meticulously uncluttered, yet hosting one obviously expensive—what? Work of art, he supposed. His face flushed as his discomfort whooshed into the stratosphere.

Opposite him, Marianne Price sank into a low white leather contraption, crossing her legs so that the long red sweater fell away revealing—Crosby averted his eyes. She was certainly middle-aged, lines like wheel spokes radiated from the corners of her large, intense dark eyes. At the same time she exuded such potent glamour that Crosby felt his mouth go dry. Older women are dangerous, he reminded himself, wrenching his eyes again away from those legs in sheer black stockings.

She leaned forward and a throb of perfume hit him. "You've brought the letters."

"Copies, yes." He handed her a manila envelope. She undid the clasp, silted the contents into her lap. She gasped theatrically.

"So many!"

"Yes."

"You realize this may take me a week or more?"

"The Department hopes you'll be able do the job sooner."

She drew dark brows together. "I don't think that's possible, unless miraculously my schedule clears."

Picking up a magnifying glass from the table at her elbow, she fanned a handful of the letters.

"Let's see. Here's one to Darling Mum, one to Dear Cynthia. The rest seem to be letters to Dear Smitty."

"Correct."

"Smitty?" Her dark eyes gleamed. "There's only one Smitty in town *I* know of."

Too late Crosby realized he should have omitted salutations and copied only the texts themselves. He swallowed.

"So these letters must be to Smitty Barker, the vet?"

"That's the party," he said reluctantly.

Marianne Price leaned forward, voice throbbing like a cello. "If that's so, our Liz can only be Smitty's wife."

"Also correct."

"The *murdered* Liz."

Crosby looked to his right and to his left. "The MLPD has not yet classified Elizabeth Barker's death as murder," he said stiffly.

As Marianne Price flopped back in her chair with a purr of satisfaction, Crosby saw that her interest in this job had suddenly shot off the charts. "Of course it was murder, Sergeant! I knew her, you see. Oh, not the way I know *Smitty*." She smiled secretly to herself, at the same time including him in her smile. "But well enough to know what she was like."

Crosby's fingers itched for his notebook, but he refused to give her the satisfaction of witnessing the fact he took her opinion seriously. Instead he said neutrally: "And what *was* she like, Mrs. Price?"

"Off the record?"

"Nothing said to an officer of the law is off the record."

"Then button my lip! Mustn't speak ill of the dead, etcetera." She paused, waiting for his curiosity to get the better of him. When it didn't, she huffed and leveled the magnifying glass again over the letters.

"You want to know whether all nine letters were written by the same person?"

"Correct."

"This one dated March 10, 1978 begins 'Dearest Smitty.' On first glance I'd say the writer is an unabashed extrovert." She passed the letter to Crosby, tapping a word with an iridescent red fingernail. "Look at those oh-so exaggerated capital letters."

Astonishingly, the term "proper noun" surfaced from some ancient English class memory; he remembered that you capitalize proper nouns. He nodded.

"*And* an egotist."

"Just because she makes big capital letters?"

"Exactly. Now look here. See how her script runs up, not down?"

"Not sure what you mean, ma'am."

"See how she slants her lines up across the page from left to right."

"That means something?"

"Of course. It's the sign of an optimist."

"Of course," mumbled Crosby, far out to sea.

"And then there's the way she crosses her t's'! But I've got to look at these letters far more closely. Shall we say five days, Sergeant? I'm being optimistic."

"If absolutely necessary."

"It is. And I don't think the Police Department asked my fee?"

"I'll make a note of that, Mrs. Price."

"I bill my services at fifteen dollars an hour."

"And how many hours do you estimate?"

"Twenty minimum."

He jotted, thrust his notebook into his pocket and rose.

"Thank you for your time, Mrs. Price. And if you can possibly expedite the job you'd be doing your local law enforcement agency a great favor."

"I promise nothing." She smiled, blew him a kiss, and shut the door firmly behind him.

Expelling breath, he headed down the pristine walk as though emerging from a dream. When he found the squad, he realized it was snowing. So he'd been right about that sky, at least. More shoveling, he thought, watching the car roof salt white. At the same time he could swear he felt a perfumed wind from the south blowing in to kiss his face.

He shook his head. "Things round here just get weirder and weirder every goddamn day."

CHAPTER THIRTEEN

"That Matilda Roth Hamilton—are we a tad pretentious or what!—promised to walk Gigi every day she's here. Barry?"

On a brand-new machine, Boycks was trying to process the credit card of a guest who, having overslept, was pacing and checking his watch every other second.

"Hold on, Nora."

In her lake house, Nora lit a cigarette, blew a stream of smoke over Gigi's head, drummed her nails on the antique farm table imported from Provence. After what seemed to her at least several eons, Boycks came back on the line.

"What can I do you for?"

"As I said, Matilda Roth—"

"Nora, why not try calling her Tillie. All her friends do."

"Then you know where I stand. Can you please locate her and remind her—"

Boyck's acute business sense and good manners kept him from slamming down the phone, and at that moment Tillie sailed past heading for the breakfast room.

"Tillie, Nora wants you to walk Gigi this morning." He held the phone at arm's length. "What do I say?"

"Say yes, but only after I've had two helpings of the house French cinnamon toast with blueberry sauce."

He reassured Nora and hung up.

"I almost forgot, there's something for you." He reached in a drawer and handed her an envelope with an uncanceled stamp. It was addressed to Matilda Roth Hamilton.

"What's this?"

"How could I possibly know? It was lying on the sideboard in the front hall when I came down this morning."

In the dining room she applied her butter knife to the envelope and pulled out a card. It showed a man wearing a suit, a tie, and silly pointed shoes. He was bearing a large red heart. Opening it she

60

read: "I think of you only twenty-four hours a day, seven days a week, three hundred and fifty-two days a year."

Whoever had sent it had added "And will forever!"

Who on earth? She realized it was Valentine's Day.

*****

Outside fog smothered the snowbanks like a large hot towel—or a Valentine lover. Fog was the result of warm air colliding with cold ground—or was it cold air colliding with warm? She never could remember. Good for the complexion, anyway.

She had indeed volunteered to walk Gigi early mornings. Hoyt painted late into the night, he'd informed her, and slept long into the morning so she had time on her hands. Yet she hadn't really expected Nora Klein to take her up on her dog walking offer. After all she, Tillie, was here on business. And they were almost total strangers. And after all, Nora had been damned rude to her under her own roof that first morning over coffee.

But a promise was a promise. And she adored Gigi. (Might it be possible to smuggle a small terrier-chihuahua mix on the plane back to New York?)

In the third block of Coolidge she stopped at the end of the drive leading to Dexter's carriage house. Two vine-laced windows faced the street, one with shade down, one with shade up. Winking at me even when he's sleeping off a long hard night, she thought. Or was the message slightly more sinister? Something like: you think you've nailed me but you're not even close.

How *did* she feel about Dexter Hoyt after three long interviews? She had expected a difficult man; all artists were difficult, weren't they? Rembrandt, Picasso, Klee? What she had not expected was an artist in love with a beautiful woman whom he painted obsessively but had never met face to face. Nor had she expected an artist convinced that the whole town believed him a murderer. Nor had she expected to walk straight into a murder investigation.

She couldn't help wondering about his sex life. She'd seen no evidence in his studio of any woman except his icon, Liz. No photographs, no whisper of perfume, no female ordering of male chaos, no tube of lipstick forgotten on the bathroom sink, no covered casserole ready for the oven. Not that she'd noticed an oven. Gay, was he? She had considered it and decided no.

At the foot of Coolidge, Mills Lake was invisible beneath a shroud of fog. Valentine's Day thaw—words from the past. Every winter her Ohio Grandmother Matilda had predicted a Valentine's Day thaw, every year she'd been right. Same with Indian Summer— mythical yet real, occurring without fail after the first hard frost of October. Indian Summer: those last smokey, wistful days before winter's sharp sword. Which had sheathed itself this February day.

She turned right, walked a long block and reached the dead end sign that announced the reign of Eleanora Klein. Do I like her? Tillie asked herself. No, she decided. Then she modified that to "maybe" and pushed the bell. Behind the door, Gigi hurled herself into a storm of barks.

"Good morning, Tillie," said Nora, nodding her inside. "Are those rabbit-fur earmuffs actually a favorite?"

"Actually they are. Ready, Gigi?"

Nora snapped leash to collar and handed over her dog. "Better not go back to New York any time soon, Tillie" (again the "Tillie"). Gigi will never forgive you. Enjoy the foggy foggy dew."

Who'd think Nora Klein would know an old English folk song.

"Off to see the Wizard," said Tillie in something of the same spirit. Nora smiled as she shut the door.

Again Tillie set out along Lake Drive. Grey, greyer and greyest: a profound hush punctuated only by the scrape of ice sliding off a roof and, out on the lake, the snarl of an invisible snowmobile. Tillie observed that Gigi choose the identical spots to pee that she had on their first walk. Well, system was all. As they approached the fire hydrant at the corner of Coolidge and Lake she almost thought she heard "Off, Fletch!" But there was no Fletch, no man wearing a plaid cap asking her to meet him downtown for coffee. Wilkie Steeves had been—a disappointment.

Downtown a few business people were keying their doors, and a hungry trio stared out the window of J. Meghan's, forking bacon and eggs and trying to wake up over coffee. Tillie and Co. turned right onto South Main, passing a bar, a laundromat and a hardware store that looked as though it might be closing sooner than later. Steve's Garage, though, was already doing a brisk business.

And then she came upon enchantment: a bridge across the mill race secured by an iron fence, though not any old iron fence. Tillie stepped back to admire the intricate mill-wheel pattern repeated and repeated until the whole bridge seemed in motion. Beneath it water foamed through the race; she remembered Barry Boycks telling her that the town was named for a sorghum mill that had stood on the edge of the mill pond in early days.

Somewhere nearby the race had to emerge downstream. Crossing Main, she passed a clutch of brick buildings that once must have been a vital part of the town and saw the new Municipal Building looming in the distance. Catching the sound of water off to her right, she found and followed a path that sloped downhill toward brush and alder until she found herself on the verge of a fast-foaming creek. Fog hung above the water—blotting the weak sun, turning trees into phantoms, probing icy fingers beneath her collar.

"Found it, didn't we, Gigi!" scooping up the dog who covered her face with kisses— "and well worth the search!" The town was only blocks away, yet she felt she'd stumbled upon an enchanted spot inhabited by only the creek, herself and the dog—though when a squirrel chirred branch to branch overhead she felt obliged to include the squirrel. Dexter Hoyt was miles away on another planet on the other side of the solar system. Granted he was a good painter. So what!

Impulsively she broke a branch from a tree, flung it into the stream and saw it whirl away downstream. Mistake. With a shrill yap, Gigi sprang from her arms and made a dash for the water. Tillie lunged for the leash, caught it, lost it, threw herself forward to grab the loop with both hands. Checked, Gigi flopped down on the stream's bank and glared at her.

It was in this elegant position—chin in snow, bottom in air—that Tillie became aware of voices. She raised her head and listened. They seemed to come from her left, down-creek, not close but not far and perhaps coming closer. She scrambled to her feet and was brushing down her coat when what had been mere sound suddenly coalesced into words.

"Pretty sure I'm in the clear," she heard a man say. *"There's not a shred of evidence."* Her eyes popped in surprise; she held her breath, straining to hear more. But now there was only the surging water. Very suddenly she knew she had to get away from this place. She felt guilty as an eavesdropper, yet could not even swear that somebody had actually spoken those words. Truly rushing water, fog and mist-wrapped trees had put her under a kind of spell. Perhaps her "enchanted spot" had imagined them for her?

She walked rapidly away from the creek, looking covertly right and left. No one. Whoever had spoken had seemingly melted, along with his or her companion, into the fog. What should she do with her new knowledge, she wondered? Then she corrected herself. Hardly knowledge. A few overheard words—and not clearly heard at that.

CHAPTER FOURTEEN

"That was one long walk," said Nora, opening the front door and nodding Tillie in. Gigi needed no invitation, speeding to the kitchen to attack her water bowl with an athlete's thirst. "Time for a cup of coffee?"

Again coffee! Tillie hesitated, not wanting to violate the rules of small-town hospitality. "Thank you, but do you have anything else hot and wet?"

"Possibly. Do you drink tea?"

"Tea would be fine," she said, craving instead a steaming mug of hot chocolate topped with three inches of whipped cream.

"The real or that awful decaffeinated stuff?"

"The awful decaffeinated stuff, please."

Nora led her through the kitchen with its marble counters, copper stove hood, tiled floor and state-of-the-art appliances to the breakfast room. No sun today: mist pressing against windows blurred the room into an impressionist work of art. Again she admired walls hung with Quimper plates ("France is my country of choice") and, overhead, the floating wooden chandelier. This time a corner cabinet also caught her appreciative eye. Circa 1800 French, guessed Tillie, and imagined a young Burgundian bride painting her cupboard cherry red, a color that had weathered over the years to faint blush rose. I could be inside a Manet, thought Tillie, or a Renoir. Nora, who claimed she paid no attention to paintings, had surrounded herself with art.

Tillie jumped up to help when she came in carrying a tray, but Nora lifted it out of her reach and set it down decisively. "Peach Sunrise for you, Brazilian dark roast for me. And ye olde sticky buns. Dog walkers deserve sticky buns."

Tillie poured from—oh god, a Limoges teapot, was it—visualizing with horrid clarity dropping it. Though actually tea was far from her thoughts. On the way back to Nora's, she'd replayed her experience at the creek over and over. What *was* it the voice had actually said? Something about *in the clear* and *no evidence*, did she

65

have that right? What she did know is that the words had suggested only one thing to her: the murder of Liz Barker.

Where, exactly, had her private scenario jumped the rails? Intrepid New York magazine writer jets to small Midwest town to interview unknown artist she plans to make famous. But said intrepid reporter finds herself involved in a murder because said artist has painted the murdered woman and claims Mills Lake believes he killed her. Following which, Intrepid finds herself definitely spooked on at least two occasions. First by what she thinks of as "the stalker"; second by "the voice." And that's not to mention a prolonged confrontation with a very drunk painter ended only by his passing inelegantly out.

With one finger Nora pushed the plate of buns across the table. Rail-thin, she looked like she'd never sunk tooth into a sweet in her life. Now she lit a cigarette, tilted back her head and shot a jet of smoke over Tillie's head.

"You act as though you've had more than an early walk, kiddo. Did something happen? Tell old Nora."

They were the first words of comfort—of *understanding*—that Tillie had heard since her arrival and she smiled gratefully.

"Nothing really."

Nora leaned forward. "But *something,* I think."

"It's going to sound so—hallucinatory."

"'Hallucinations deeply interest me."

"Do they?"

"I'm a psychiatrist, Tillie. Retired, yes. But like the daughter who's your daughter the rest of her life, a psychiatrist's a psychiatrist the rest of hers."

"Okay, then." She spread her hands on the table. "Gigi and I walked downtown and came to a bridge by the Legion building—you know, that fence above a race that spills out of the pond."

Nora nodded.

"So then I wondered, you know, where does this water go? We crossed Main and walked down—is it Water Street?—until I heard rushing water again. I found a path, took it, and there it was, buried behind trees and brush: the race just barely settling down into a creek, you know?"

"I do know. It's called Mills Creek and it flows all the way to the Rock River. Around here, hard as you may try, you can't get away from the Rock River. And then?"

"And then we were about to head back when I heard a voice."

Nora raised dark eyebrows and stabbed out her Parliament in a silver ashtray.

"A man's voice, I think. Obviously talking to someone."

"Or soliloquizing—"

She'd taken two Shakespeare classes at NYU. "I don't think so."

"And what did this voice say?"

"I only caught a few words."

Nora poured herself a second cup, looked at its contents with disgust. "Why does the coffee *I* make turn to mud after the first cup? Smitty says his coffee maker's good for ten cups cup. And these few words, what were they?"

"I think they might have been *in the clear* and *no evidence.*"

They sat in silence watching Gigi circle until she dropped into her bed. Nora plucked another Parliament from a silver case.

"Must you?"

"*I beg your pardon?*"

"Sorry, but cigarette smoke has always made me slightly ill."

"This happens to be my house, Tillie."

"I am completely aware of that."

Nora replaced the cigarette. Her face was stoney. "So you heard words. What did they suggest to you?"

Tillie shifted in her chair. "This is crazy, but I thought right away of the murder. You know: Icehenge, the lady in ice."

Nora's smooth dark brows shot almost to her hairline "*Really?*"

"Really. After all, it hasn't been that long since she was discovered. Even I've picked up vibes suggesting people not only constantly think about it but that it's seriously freaking them out."

Nora nodded. "Perhaps. But back to the creek, the suspense is killing me. Who was this mysterious man in the fog?"

"I don't know," lied Tillie. No: only half lied; she wasn't really sure.

"No wonder, I suppose. You haven't met many people, have you? Though you've met Smitty. Could it"—she wrinkled her nose—"could it have been Smitty speaking?"

Smitty Barker? Why would Nora even think it could be her friend!

"No, no," Tillie said positively, "For one thing, Dr. Barker's voice is pitched rather high for a big man, rather charming, really."

"Then let's play Sherlock. Who else do you know?"

"Hoyt, of course, but it couldn't have been Hoyt, he doesn't get out of bed until ten." She ticked off her fingers. "Barry Boycks—again no. But wait a minute, last night I met a man at the Manse. Ted somebody."

"Offhand, I can think of three Teds I know."

"This one was lanky, blondish. Signet ring that could put out your eye."

"A woman with him, petite, white hair?"

"Yes."

"That would be Ted Gage."

Tillie took another sip of lukewarm peach tea and set down her cup with finality. "Actually, it *might* have been him. It was a carrying kind of voice and Ted's voice certainly carried." She felt not a shred of guilt implicating the man who'd told her that people knew Dexter Hoyt "to their sorrow."

"All right, Watson, but what about motive? He has to have had a motive."

"I can't possibly guess. I only met him last night."

"True." Nora reached for her case, inhaling as though a lit cigarette was already between her lips, retracted her hand. "I might be able to suggest one."

"Really?"

"No proof, mind you, though I do credit myself with some psychological insight. My impression is that there was definitely something between Liz Barker and Ted Gage."

Tillie heaved a sigh. She'd thought she had a straight-forward mission: an article about Dexter Hoyt. But then she'd insisted on taking Gigi for a walk. "What kind of something?"

"I don't wish to speculate. You know how small towns thrive on gossip, innuendo, rumor. One has to pick one's way carefully through the muck."

"That's why I live in New York."

"Which is only the same gossip, rumor and innuendo multiplied eight million times. But back to the famous foggy creek. Is there anybody else you think it might be?"

Tillie hesitated. "Well, there's Adam Quick."

"Ah, Adam."

"You say that as though—" Tillie hesitated to complete Nora's thought.

"As though Adam would be my first choice?"

"Surely he's not!"said Tillie, shocked.

Nora only smiled suggestively.

"But why?"

"Oh, I don't know. Arrogant. Possessive. Never forgave Liz for divorcing him, and I mean *never*. And that's neither local rumor nor gossip, but fact."

"You really suspect Professor Quick of murdering Liz Barker?"

"Not exactly, but I wouldn't be surprised if he did. Frankly, I don't know why he hasn't been arrested long ago. On the other hand, I can't imagine what he'd be doing down at the creek on a cold winter morning. Or who he'd be talking to if he were. Adam doesn't have a friend in town."

"Poor man," said Tillie sincerely.

"Though wait." Nora tapped Tillie's hand with a shiny nail. "Maybe we're going at this the wrong way. Maybe we should think spatially, if that's the word. Who might naturally be down at the creek early in the morning?"

"I don't know. Someone with a business nearby? The restaurant was open. And a garage—"

"Yes, Steve's opens at seven."

"Steeves?" Tillie frowned.

"Not the City Manager," said Nora, seeing her confusion. "And not that I'm suggesting the garage owner, Steve. He's so honest he still charges fifteen dollars for an oil change *and* rotating tires. But what about Fish Hatchery employees? Not that I've ever met any, do they exist, I wonder? And then there's the Municipal Building right down the street—"

"Housing the Police Department," said Tillie, proud of her Mills Lake knowledge, "*and* the Main Street Program *and* Light and Water and who knows what upstanding community bureau else."

"The Chamber of Commerce, for one." Nora chewed her lip. "And of course the City Manager. Come to think of it, I *have* heard that Wilk's the earliest bird at his desk—"

Tillie shoved back her chair.

"Hold on, child, we may be getting somewhere. Let's keep focused on that voice. For instance, was it an *educated* voice?"

"So few words to go by—"

"But surely the words *in the clear* and *no evidence* are educated?"

"I suppose so and, yes, I'd say it was an educated voice though I really don't know what that means. But I don't see where that gets us. Most municipal employees are educated, aren't they?"

"Not necessarily. What I'm trying to get at—was it a kind of public-speaking voice?"

Tillie rose. "I've got to go, Nora. Thanks so much for letting me take Gigi. We had a good walk."

"Off so soon? We were just getting interesting."

"I have an appointment with Hoyt at nine."

Nora edged back a black cashmere sweater cuff to check her watch. "Dex never, but never, rises before ten."

"This morning he does," said Tillie. "Finish your morning mud, dear Nora. I'll let myself out."

70

CHAPTER FIFTEEN

Of course Hoyt wouldn't roll out of bed before ten, but Tillie urgently needed to leave the witness chair. Nora had been kind, kinder than Tillie had imagined she could be. But she needed time to think, to assess her feelings, to recuperate. Strange word—recuperate—but accurate. Her morning walk with Gigi had shaken her; she wanted to understand why.

The fog had lifted and the world looked very matter-of-fact. Hard to believe that a mere two hours ago she and Gigi, exploring the mill race, had heard Wilk Steeve's' voice. Yes: she'd decided it must have been the City Manager speaking. Though by now she would hesitate to swear in a court of law to what or whom she had heard.

No place to go in this charming town (officially a city) except Waterhouse, home of espresso addicts, *Wisconsin State Journal* readers, and fans of the world's best blueberry scones, as advertised on a hand-written notice taped to the cash register. Tillie didn't for a moment believe they could compete with the scones at Victor's Forty-Fifth Street *patisserie*, but she was willing to put them to the test. Anything to ground herself in something familiar, something everyday.

She ordered and paid at the tiny counter, carried a steaming mug and a warm scone wrapped in a brown paper napkin to one of the tables in back. Shrugging off her coat and springing the ear muffs, she unzipped her briefcase and took out the legal pad. She needed to review the notes she'd taken, needed to re-focus on the assignment that had brought her here.

Leafing through them, she was startled to read her private jottings about Hoyt himself. "Paranoid," she had noted. "Defensive, a buried but decided charm, probably a genius, definitely OCD, closet homosexual?" Had she really dared to write those words? Who did she think she was—Dr. Eleanora Klein!

"Tillie?"

She looked up from her notes. A woman wrapped in a scarf that almost obscured her silver hair waved from a nearby table.

"You probably don't remember me," she said with a diffident smile. "Ferry Manse a couple of nights ago?"

"I do remember." Tillie hesitated. She needed to prep for her Hoyt appointment, yet she also wanted to talk to Sue Ellen. "Please join me if you'd like."

Collecting her belongings, Sue Ellen slid into a chair opposite, setting down her coffee then redistributing her load over two chairs.

"Apologies for the gear. It's in-service day, which means kids are off and teachers don't have to report until nine-thirty." She consulted a man-sized watch strapped to a delicate wrist. "Actually I've got a whole half-hour. So, tell me, how do you like the Manse?"

Considering that Sue Ellen and Ted were fireplace friends of Barry Boycks, Tillie felt she had only one possible answer.

"I like it. Cosy, tons of Victorian atmosphere. Maybe a tad too many teddy bears?"

Sue Ellen snorted. "I *know.* I told Barry to go easy on the teddy bears. Obviously he ignored me."

"*Are* teddy bears Victorian, anyway?"

"Oh, absolutely. Look at the illustrations of any nineteenth-century children's book. The kids are always dragging teddy bears around."

"I *loved* the Pooh stories, did you?"

"Milne's later, but yes: *loved.*"

"Not to pry, but Ted—or is it *Teddy?*"—they both reared back hooting—" your partner? That *is* prying, sorry. No need to answer."

"Ted's my husband, actually. Yes, 1 know: we're not wearing rings, but we are married, for what that's worth. We met at one of the martini clubs."

"Martini clubs?"

"Oh, Mills Lake's more sophisticated than you'd think." Her mouth quirked. "Actually, after round two there's nothing sophisticated about a martini club at all."

Tillie smiled, but could not forget Ted's remark that people knew Hoyt "to their sorrow." Yet now she knew Sue Ellen and Ted were married, how could she bring it up—or the fact that it had hurt and disturbed her. You didn't criticize the husband of someone you barely knew. Could she introduce the topic neutrally? She leaned forward with a smile.

"You say that you and Hoyt are neighbors?"

"Roughly." Sue Ellen looked away. "Not next-door or anything," she added.

"Of course I'd never use this in my article, but I can't help wondering what your husband meant when he said that people knew Dex "to their sorrow.""

Sue Ellen flamed to the roots of her silver hair. "It's so awful he said that to you who've come all the way from New York to write about him. Sometime Ted can be—well, tactless doesn't describe it."

"So there's no truth in his remark?"

Sue Ellen winced. "Hoyt's local creditors might know him to their sorrow, I suppose."

Tillie leaned back, relieved. If that was all! Struggling artists notoriously did not pay their debts; it was almost expected of them.

As though she sensed a shift in Tillie's mood, Sue Ellen leaned across the table. "So how's the article coming?"

Tillie hesitated. "It's coming. I want to stress again that I'd very much appreciate your input. And, not incidentally, I totally agree with what you said the other night: that Dexter Hoyt is a professional. More than a professional, in my book. A genius."

"I knew you were enthusiastic otherwise you wouldn't be here. I'm still curious, though. Do you mind saying what tack you're taking?"

"Tack?"

"What angle. I mean, are you stressing small town-boy-makes-good-despite-humble-origins? Or loading it with local color—if you can credit Mills Lake with that. Or focusing on the paintings in an art critic kind of way?"

Why do you care? wondered Tillie, at the same deciding that giving Sue Ellen a general idea of her approach wouldn't compromise her work.

"Well, there'll be local color—in moderation. But really the whole point of the article is discovering a genius, which means focusing on the work. I do find, though, that I'm spending a lot of time analyzing the paintings. I didn't plan on doing it that way, but the minute I walked into his studio, some of the paintings seemed to reach out and grab me, shouting 'Understand me!'"

Sue Ellen hesitated. "Thing is, though, that kind of analysis can be so— negative. I mean critics never look at a painting and say, 'He's good to his mother,' or 'He pays his bills on time.' No, it's always the darkest and dirtiest stuff they can dredge up—" She nodded at a watercolor hanging on a near wall. "That painting, for instance. It's a simple landscape with birch trees and a stream, right? But that won't satisfy a critic, a critic's got to say it depicts the artist's longing for his mother's womb or his subconscious desire to escape into oblivion—" She raised her mug to her lips, grimaced. "Coffee's cold, that's what I get for sounding off. Look, I've no business—"

"No, it's fine," said Tillie. But was it? She felt assaulted and at the same guilty. She had "dredged up" some pretty dark meanings out of Hoyt's paintings, but she didn't consider them dirty, only human.

Sue Ellen checked her watch. "I have to go. I didn't mean to rant on, honestly. Good luck with what you're doing, I mean it. Maybe we'll meet again?" Slinging the back-pack over her shoulder, she headed for the door.

"Wait !" Tillie caught up and steered her into an alcove filled with children's books and toys. "Look, I'm on Dexter's side, you must realize that. But I'd like to know: why do you care?"

Sue Ellen freed her arm. "I care about artists, that's all. Including Dexter Hoyt."

CHAPTER SIXTEEN

When Hoyt opened the door Tillie was startled to see he was smiling. He was also wearing a jacket so old that the brown leather had turned white with fine cracks. He had also wrapped his neck in a yellow wool scarf full of holes. She had never imagined Dexter Hoyt in outdoor clothes; he seemed a man of interiors.

"Something different today," he said. "*If* Matilda Roth Hamilton will permit."

"'I guess I'll permit," she said cautiously.

"Then we're going for a drive."

She followed him round the corner of the carriage house to a makeshift garage she'd never noticed. Putting shoulder to wood, he coaxed back a sliding door to reveal a cave hosting an old pea-green Volkswagen. "This is Arabella," he said, sweeping a bow of introduction, then escorting her to the passenger door. Tillie could have sworn it was fastened on with duct tape, but dismissed her impression as fantastic. Arabella did not start on first try, nor on the second. When she finally sputtered into life, Dexter shot down the long drive in reverse. Save me, muttered Tillie, reaching for her seat belt. There was no seatbelt.

They headed out of town on what Hoyt informed her was county highway B, passing the frozen expanse of Mills Lake on the left, then a rash of development, and finally reaching gently-rolling farmland.

"Mr. Hoyt," said Tillie, "I need to know where we're going."

"You're a control freak, know that?"

"I do and I don't apologize."

"Anyway—and for god's sake use my first name. This Mr. Hoyt business is driving me crazy; I feel I have to live up to some image you have of me. Anyway, you keep saying you want background, so here comes background. I grew up on a farm outside of Madison. Bet you didn't guess my parents were farmers, did you?"

"I did not."

"Well, they were, and damn successful. Plus my dad was a genius, you know? He invented a machine to pipe silage into dairy barns and feed an entire herd in ten minutes flat. Took out a patent and sold it all over the Midwest, made a wad of money." He slammed the wheel with the flat of his hand. "Hell of a wad."

"Which is why you're driving an old VW that sounds like a dying goat?"

He threw back his head in noiseless laughter. "Behold the prodigal son, Tillie. Only no wineskins when I returned; in fact I was forbidden to return under any circumstances. My younger sister and her husband inherited all the dough because they went into farming. She was the golden child. Artists didn't run in the family—as I was informed on a daily basis."

The VW shuddered as he braked to turn onto a desolate road. Treeless, it wound inward and upward, circling the base of low hills. Finally, as the snowy terrain leveled off, she saw off to the left an imposing compound of white buildings.

"The farm?"

"The farm."

"But you're forbidden to return under any circumstances—"

"That was then. Dad died in 1973. Put a gun to his head. Dying of liver cancer, decided not to serve his sentence."

"I'm sorry."

"Don't be, he was a bastard."

"And your mother?"

"Good old Nanette. She's still alive and rotting in a swanky nursing home that's gobbling up two hundred bucks a day. So there you have it. One of my sibs got a chunk of cash because she married and moved far away. My older sister and I got booted out of the nest."

"Do I *have* to include all this?"

He shot her a glance out of the corner of his eye. "I don't know, *do* you?"

76

The cold living room smelled of damp and loneliness. He crossed the carpet and yanked open a bank of brown drapes to reveal a huge fifties picture window staring out on snowy fields.

"Nobody lives here then?"

"Nobody. No electricity, no water. The house is for sale, unlisted. There've been three or four inquiries, no offers."

Tillie shivered. "It's sad. I hate empty houses."

"You wouldn't have liked it full, trust me."

"That bad? All of them?"

He frowned. "Not all. Mother was a saint, I worshipped her. My older sister, she took care of me when Mom was ill, which was a lot of the time. They were the good guys."

"And you?"

He quirked his eyebrows at her. "I leave that to you to decide."

She turned from the window to a room not empty at all, but burdened with overstuffed couches and brown vinyl Barcaloungers that matched those depressing drapes. An expensive console television set dating from (she guessed) the Seventies dominated the room. Not a painting on the walls. Poor Dexter. On the other hand every table bristled with framed photographs. She sighed and pulled out her notebook. "One of those homes whose world-view begins and ends with family photos and the TV screen," she jotted. Again: poor Dexter.

Tucking her chin deeper into her fur collar—cold as a mausoleum, this house—she drifted toward the photographs. The largest on display was a gold-framed wedding portrait that, from the style of the woman's clothes, dated from the 1930s. Father and Mother Hoyt, of course. Mother, with black hair and truculent mouth looking much like Dexter; Father lean, hard and aloof. She moved on to photos documenting Hoyt children: kids graduating from tricycles to bicycles to what was obviously Dexter's first car. (Good god, could it be Arabella?) Somehow the sequence depressed her if only because it seemed to be the story of every American family.

She paused at another table to pick up a fake-gold frame. The photo it contained was not good: three rather out-of-focus grinning teens in swim suits on the shore of a lake. She recognized Dexter on the left—unruly dark shoulder-length hair, arm flung about the shoulders of the girl next to him. Looking more closely, however, she saw that his eyes were locked on the third of the trio, a fair-haired teen in a bikini smoldering behind Raybans yet cool even at the beach. Tillie inhaled sharply. She'd seen that girl's older self in half a dozen Hoyt paintings.

Liz Barker.

"Who gave you permission to snoop the family art?"

Looking up, Tillie didn't much like the Dexter Hoyt now standing over her. She set the picture back on the table.

"You did," she said defiantly.

"But not to take inventory."

"Look, Mr. Hoyt—Dexter—you're the one who brought me out here for background."

"But you're the one who wanted it."

"No apologies for that. Background explains foreground. Anyway, this photograph interests me, so bear with me for a while. That's you on the left—"

He flicked a finger at the boy in the photo. "Dexter Hoyt in his unwashed hippie days. I was starting a beard."

"So glad you didn't finish it."

"But I did."

"The face in the middle I don't recognize, but this one on the right I *do*."

"That's weird, you being from New York and all."

"You know what I mean. This is the woman you paint all the time, the woman out your window. The woman with snake."

"So if it is?"

Tillie swung round to face him, feeling excited, puzzled and betrayed all at once. "You told me you'd never met her, only seen her once or twice in her back yard. I've got it right here in my note-book—"

"I did see her once or twice in her back yard."

"Yes, but you'd known her—" she tapped the face under glass—"since you were what—sixteen?"

"Fifteen."

Tillie took the plunge. "And you were crazy about her, weren't you."

"There we are not going."

She opened her mouth to protest, shut it. He was right. She had no business prying into his past. Except—except that his paintings of Elizabeth Barker were central to his art and that his art was the most important thing in her life right now. But he'd lied to her about not knowing his muse.

"Fine," she said, returning the photo to the table whose only other ornament was a hideous red and yellow ceramic lamp. (Poor Dexter.) Then on impulse she picked it up again.

"The one in the middle, she looks familiar somehow— though how I can say that when I'm a stranger in town I've no idea. Who is she, Dexter?"

Dexter was at the picture window about to close the brown waterfall. "My older sister," he said over his shoulder. "You don't know her."

"*Don't* close those drapes." She brought the photograph to the light. "What's your sister's name?"

"Oh, Sister Sue, please be true," he sang, ridiculously off-key.

Sue. She looked again at the teen-ager posed between Dexter and Liz; at the pretty face with its up-tilted nose, the shy smile. The wet boy-cut hair slicked back from the face. Suddenly it hit her.

Sue Ellen. Sue Ellen in front of the fire, Sue Ellen of the youthful face and prematurely white hair. (Hoyt's white streak multiplied?) Sue Ellen who'd said to her just this morning, "I believe in giving artists a chance." Tillie was so excited she stuttered.

"But I know your sister! I had coffee with her just this morning—" Words tumbled out.

He looked down pointedly at her hand on his arm; she removed it.

"Well, well. So you've met Sue Ellen."

"Yes, and now I understand! She talked about artists, she said you were the real thing. She was talking about her brother."

The brown curtains grated on their rods.

"*Don't* ! I need to see."

"We'll talk about it in the car, Matilda Roth Hamilton." She realized he always used her full name when he disliked her. "Put the picture back where it belongs."

She obeyed. He propelled her roughly to the door. They stepped out into the winter-dead farmland.

"She believes in you, you know."

Dexter wrenched open his door, leaving her to struggle with the passenger side. The car was deathly cold, twice as cold as the dead house, windshield smothered in frost. He fired the engine. Again Arabella coughed, died, coughed. Oh, god, prayed Tillie, let me not be stranded out here in this wilderness with Dexter Hoyt. I'm a New Yorker, I don't drive a car, I hate the cold. I'm a city wimp freaked out by even this small rural adventure.

In answer to her prayer, Arabella gasped into life. The wipers flopped back and forth, not making a dent in the frost.

"Shit."

He got out and clawed at the glaze with his bare fingers, but he'd forgotten to turn off the wipers. Striking the windshield with a fist, he crawled back into the car. Nothing he'd done had improved visibility. Arabella lurched down the drive, Dexter squinting through a clear patch the size of a beer coaster.

"You can't drive like this, you can't see." Should she jump out, hitch-hike back to Mills Lake?

"*Would* you relax!"

He shot into the road without a glance for traffic. She couldn't blame him for wanting to leave in hurry, though. Farm houses were supposed to be comfy-cosy, weren't they? Pot-bellied stoves, harvest tables, gingham curtains, apple pies cooling on window sills. *His* family's farm house looked like a funeral parlor furnished in exceptionally bad taste.

He didn't want to talk, that was obvious: every time she turned to him with a question on her lips he hunched a shoulder

80

against her. Except for the scrape of wipers, they drove in a silence Tillie felt helpless to break. Yet she discovered she couldn't drop the subject of Sue Ellen.

"Your sister really does believe in you," she ventured again, remembering how she'd demanded of Sue Ellen that morning *Why do you care?* Her question had now dramatically been answered. Sue Ellen cared because she was the loving older sister who'd watched out for little Dex, mothered him when Mother Hoyt was ill.

Finally he spoke. "Possibly Sue Ellen does believe in me as an artist. But then there's her other belief." He looked at her at last. "Want to know what that is, Matilda?" When she didn't answer, he threw back his head and laughed for the first time since they'd met. "This is for the record—*yours*. My sister believes I murdered Liz Barker. She believes it so completely she hasn't spoken to me since the day old Liz showed up in ice. I can take the rest of the natives being that stupid, but it's fuckin' hard to take her."

They drove the remaining miles in silence. Tillie unrolled her coat cuffs and tucked them around her freezing hands. What could she say, what could be said? Then she remembered.

"I don't think you murdered anybody, Dexter."

"Thanks. But how would *you* know?"

"Because I heard the real murderer's confession."

CHAPTER SEVENTEEN

At four p.m. Bill & Helen's emanated the holy calm that exists for those brief expectant moments before rush hour begins. Helen conveyed to her customer his regular gin gimlet with three olives skewered on a red pick. Laying down a napkin advertising Coors, she set his drink in the exact middle of the square. He smiled his appreciation. Soon customers would be shouting for Millers and brandy Old Fashioneds over an ad-choked TV that nobody paid any attention to except on Packers game days.

This is why I come early, thought Wilk Steeves. Did he have a reputation as a drinker? Since he habitually returned to his office to work from five until seven, he didn't think so. Mostly he didn't care. Neither did he know why he favored gin gimlets, except that they were the favored drink of Raymond Chandler's Phillip Marlowe in *The Long Goodbye,* his favorite noir. Also his ex drank gin gimlets. He hoped his choice had nothing to do with Chrystal, though he suspected it had, or at least with his (badly) failed marriage.

The door opened and a tall man he didn't know strode in, ordered a tap beer, circled the bar and slid onto the next stool but one. The tall man nodded and clinked Wilk's glass.

"Cheers. Bill Byrd here."

"Steeves," said Wilk grudgingly.

"City Manager Steeves?"

"That's me."

"Thought I recognized you. I want you to know that the way you handled that City Council zoning squabble was right-on."

So few people followed Council business that Wilk was lost for words.

"Also we guys sure appreciated your willingness to lead off the Henge unveiling on Carnival morning."

"Thanks," he said. The man's name had finally clicked. Byrd: one of the men responsible for Icehenge. The fatal Henge as it turned out, a reputation that, though the structure had been dismantled, would probably never go away. "Your Henge was picked up nationally, did you know? My phone never quit ringing."

"That's thanks to Devon. He was all over the publicity angle, though he hardly expected it to take off the way it did. We made the Today Show, Nightline *and* Good Morning America."

"As well as every TV station in Wisconsin—"

"Though Dev admits the national coverage turned out to be not so much about Henge but what was inside it."

Wilk allowed the last of his Gimlet to slide down his throat. "Tough luck, I agree. But the interest was definitely there before that happened."

"Depends how you look at it. Are the police any closer to figuring out how Ice Lady wound up in our masterpiece?"

Wilk tapped the rim of his glass with his finger signaling for a refill—a first. He turned to Bird. "Somehow," he said carefully, "people continue to confuse the City Manager with the police department. You did just now. Why is that, do you know?"

Byrd took an extra-long swig of his brew. "Maybe because you run every game in town?"

Wilk banged a fist on the bar. "Untrue!" Over-reacting, he knew immediately. But these were tense days.

"Whoa! No criticism, quite the reverse. Compared to our last city manager, you are ace."

"Thanks," he said wearily.

"But speaking of the police, what's going on?'

Wilk smiled automatically as Helen installed a second pristine gimlet on a second pristine square, but the magic had vanished. Other customers had stormed his sanctuary and were yanking the pinball machine's bells and whistles. And Byrd had ordered another beer.

"Actually it's been only thirteen days."

"Seems like a year though, doesn't it?"

"To me it seems like twenty."

Bill laughed. "To me too. Want to know why?"

Wilk covertly checked his watch. Overdue back in his office, his peace and quiet shattered. He sighed.

"Sure."

Byrd slid over to the next seat.

"Well, I always thought it funny." His voice was so low that Wilk had to cup an ear to hear him. "Originally Devon wanted Henge down at the end of Coolidge Street, mainly because Devon *lives* on Coolidge. But Quinn was dead against that. He argued for Bartel's Beach where there's parking and easy access to the lake. And Bartel's is close to downtown and Winter Carnival locales.

"Well, I didn't like it and neither did Devon. Why? Because Bartel's is the hub of most Carnival events—plus the main snow-mobile access to the lake. I mean, did we really want Henge up-staged by snowmobiles?"

"I see the problem."

"But Quinn *could not see it*. How one man wore down the rest I don't know, but he did."

Wilk extracted a ten and a five from his wallet and tucked the bills under his glass.

"Hear me out, City Manager. What I'm saying is: *"Why would Quinn Hale insist on that spot?"*

"I can't guess." The second gimlet had not been a good idea; his head felt as if it were floating three feet above his shoulders.

"Well, I can." Bird threw back his head to quaff his beer, adam's apple bobbing above his buttoned plaid shirt collar. He set down his glass. *"I'm thinking Quinn felt the body would be there."*

Steeves stared at him incredulously. "Look, Bill," he said, dropping his voice, like Byrd's, to a whisper. *"Nobody* can know where a body dumped into a lake will end up."

"I didn't say *knows,* I said *suspects*. Quinn's a lake scientist, you know. Water quality, temps, wind factors—he's on top of all that."

"Even if he guesses where a body might surface—I don't buy *knows* for one minute—so what? What good does it do him?"

Byrd looked over his shoulder, leaned closer.

84

"I figure maybe Quinn saw something suspicious out on the lake last fall. He's out there with his boat, you know, until it ices over. Maybe he saw a boat long after boats usually go into dock for the winter. Maybe he actually saw the act. So he's got this knowledge—a body's been dumped into the lake."

"Then why doesn't he go straight to the police?"

"Quinn's a real cautious guy, needs lots of evidence before he acts on anything. Then around Christmas last year Devon comes up with the Icehenge idea and enlists me, Quinn, and my son Calvin to help."

Wilk thought he might be getting Byrd's drift.

"Quinn figures there's been a murder, so his scientific mind goes into high gear. What if we hack ice slabs from the place he calculates the body might be? What if the corpse is revealed at the Winter Carnival in front of a crowd? And what if that crowd includes the murderer—"

Wilk was off his bar stool and into his parka.

"Good to meet you, Bill, sorry, I've got to run." He turned back. "And just who would that murderer be?"

Byrd laid a finger on his lips.

"Quinn would keep that to himself. As I said, he's a very cautious guy."

CHAPTER EIGHTEEN

The trip to the family farm that had started happily enough had blown up when Tillie mentioned Sue Ellen. No chance now that Dexter Hoyt would open up to her. Yet there was still so much she needed to discover—and the clock was ticking relentlessly.

For some reason their excursion had reminded Tillie of her breakup with her boyfriend Ben. It was Sunday, they'd planned a stroll through Central Park and a glass of champagne at the Plaza afterward; but the stroll had turned out to be a nightmare. Stuffed to bursting by half the population of New York, Central Park steamed like a jungle. Children screamed, cyclists ran them off the paths, picnickers blared boomboxes and tossed beer cans. Finally on the path to Belvedere Castle they'd faced each other.

"I can't do this anymore." Tillie.

"You can't, I sure can't either." Ben.

"I'm referring to our Sundays together." Tillie.

"So am I." Ben, whose name, she'd discovered to her delight when she believed herself in love with him, was not Benjamin but the more elegant Benedict.

And that had been, quite brutally, the end of a three-year romance. She didn't know why she was thinking of it now.

Hoyt dropped her at the end of his drive. She summoned her manners.

"Thank you so much for showing me your family farm. That was special and I really appreciate it." When he didn't respond she got out of the car and shut the door. Then she remembered, walked round the car and tapped on his window. He cranked it down.

"The photographer had to postpone, but he's coming tomorrow."

"What?"

"The photographer. Tomorrow."

He stared at her blankly.

"You know, Nathan Ely."

"Shit."

"Photographing your paintings, Mr. Hoyt, is part of our deal."

"Shit."

"Tomorrow at ten. You'll be here, won't you?"

"Well fuck, Matilda, where else do I have to go?"

To hell? thought Tillie. "Right then. See you tomorrow."

The mild late afternoon had turned blustery, a slate sky again promising snow. She turned up her fur collar. Though only four in the afternoon, she began to think of where she'd could get her dinner. She also decided she must phone New York and coax her editor Jim Jesko to underwrite a couple of extra days in Mills Lake.

As for Dexter Hoyt, nothing had been explained to her satisfaction. Why hadn't he asked about her "real murderer confession"? Why hadn't she tackled him about Sue Ellen believing he murdered Liz Barker? Every nail she thought she'd hammered solid over the past four days he had somehow managed to work loose.

She trudged down Coolidge against a bitter wind. Out of breath by the time she reached the Manse, she was greeted at the door by Boycks. His smile was almost coy.

"Genleman callah, Matilda," he purred in an imitation Southern drawl, "waitin' on y'all in the parlah."

"Thanks, Tennessee."

Pulling off her ear muffs, she ran her hands through her hair, turning it into a fiery halo—her idea of making herself presentable. She noted her heart was thudding, and not from the walk.

A tall, narrow man in the olive-drab parka that seemed to be standard-issue Mills Lake male winter wear stood at the bay window, rocking on his heels as he knuckled a tattoo on the pane. She stopped, confused. Adam Quick turned to greet her.

"You wonder why I'm here."

Tillie repressed a sarcastic comeback. "Yes.

"I have to confess I wasn't strictly honest with you the other day."

"Oh?"

"When I told you I couldn't tell you anything more about Hoyt and his paintings."

"Why did you lie?"

He reared back, offended; then laughed. "You confuse a lie with a small sin of omission."

"Small, yet still a sin."

"Look, we got off on the wrong foot the other evening—my fault, I'm sure. I'm here to apologize and ask if you'd like to come for a drink and a bite to eat. Strictly to the benefit of your article, of course."

She heard Nora Klein saying, "I don't know why he hasn't been arrested for the murder." After all, she could be wrong about the voice at the creek, in fact probably *was* wrong. It was also possible that Quick had been the person following her that night; she was convinced now that she'd been shadowed. She shivered. Yet perversely she felt excited.

"I'd like to."

"Any preference?"

"Waterhouse, I guess."

"Waterhouse is for hippies."

"Hippies in Mills Lake?"

"You'd be surprised. Anyway, I have a better idea."

He drove a Pinto crusted so thick with road salt she couldn't tell its color. An unlikely car, she thought, for a professor who "brought in millions" to his university. He braked cautiously for three blocks, backed painstakingly into an empty parking slot. She was out of the Pinto before he came round to open her door. They stood in front of one of the two-story nineteenth-century brick buildings that characterized the downtown. Below a finely carved cornice overhead a neon sign flashed "Bill & Helen's Eats & Drinks."

"This is your better idea?" said Tillie doubtfully.

"Great food." He opened the door and formally ushered her in.

Jukebox, two pinball machines, a small corner TV staring like Cyclops, an outsized padded bar shaped like a horseshoe. Two customers hunched on stools staring into their drinks. Inside the horseshoe a grey-haired woman in a gold and green sweatshirt was swigging a beer. She looked up and saw them; reared back, aimed and pulled an imaginary trigger.

Quick flew his hand over his head. "Don't shoot!"

"I always shoot customers who don't show for a month."

"No, but listen. Shooting customers is counter-productive. Besides, Helen, you know you love me."

He guided Tillie to the curve of the bar, trailed by Helen and her beer bottle.

"So what'll it be, Professor?"

"Helen, this is Matilda Roth Hamilton from New York."

"Good to meet you, Matilda."

"She's here to do an article about our local hero."

"And who would that be?"

"Dexter Hoyt."

Helen snorted. "Ain't *my* hero."

"Why not?"

"He don't come in no more."

"Not everyone has my sophisticated taste."

She threw back her head and roared.

"So what'll it be for drinks, Professor?"

"The usual for me. Tillie?"

But Tillie was dumb with amazement. Never could she have imagined Quick trading banter with a bartender, even if that tender co-owned the bar. Yelling "Don't shoot," protesting "Helen, you know you love me"—they were behavior and words so out of character as to make her doubt her senses.

"So what can I do for you, Miss Matilda?"

What did the locals drink? Diplomatically she should order a Wisconsin beer—Helen's brand if she could discover it—but she didn't know any.

"I'll have a chardonnay, please," she said finally.

"*Shardonay?*" Helen stared in disbelief.

Quick laughed. "She means a brandy Old-Fashioned sweet," he corrected.

"More like it." Helen applied herself to the ranks of bottles stashed beneath the bar.

Tillie reached for the ever-present notebook, uncapped her Bic. After all, Quick had promised a lunch that would benefit her article.

"About that 'minor sin,' Professor," she began, "what more do you have to tell me about Hoyt's paintings?"

"Could you possibly bring yourself to call me Adam?"

"That isn't the point, is it?" Biting her pen, she studied him. He was thin—something the bulky off-white Aran Island sweater he was wearing only emphasized. He didn't look like a murderer, though she could readily imagine him toying with life in some sinister nuclear lab. "I will," she said reluctantly, "if you can possibly bring yourself to call me Tillie."

He frowned and she realized he disliked sassy women.

"All right. What I didn't tell you, *Tillie*, is that the Chicago Art Museum is giving your Dexter a major exhibit this summer."

Her smile collapsed, she turned to him in dismay. "But I know that already, he told me himself. And by the way, he's definitely not *my* Dexter."

Helen set down their drinks with the care of a midwife delivering babies. A martini for Quick, for Tillie a squat glass with a slice of orange clapped on its rim and something fluorescently red lurking in its depths. She recognized it as the libation Boycks had offered her at his fireside.

"Running a tab, Professor?"

"Right. What tempts you, Tillie?"

"What do you have?" she asked, looking around for a menu.

"Bill and Helen's is famous for burgers, more famous for ribs."

Tillie shuddered. "I'm sorry," she said, feeling very New Yorkishly vegan, "I don't eat anything that has eyes."

Helen rolled hers.

Adam Quick was amused. "To each her own," he said. "I'll have the Bleu Burger and fries."

"Like always. You, Tillie, who don't eat nothin' with eyes?"

"An order of fries, please."

"That's it?"

"And a small salad, please."

"*Salad?*"

"She'll have the slaw," corrected Quick. She intercepted the glance he and Helen exchanged.

Great, Tillie—managing to strike out first time at bat. At the same time she could picture herself back in the East Village in their booth at Celeste, regaling Kathryn and Lisa with stories of this trip. She would paint Mills Lake as both exotic and benighted-heartland-America. She could hardly wait to escape the reality.

"Besides the Chicago exhibit—old news, I'm afraid—can you tell me more about Dexter's paintings?"

Upper lip testing his martini, he turned to her, scanning her face as though calculating whether she was worthy of his news.

"All right, this. Do you know that Dex has a rich patron?"

Tillie jotted down the information. Then, looking up: "But I thought that was you."

"No, I'm talking rich-rich."

"He hasn't mentioned any rich patron,"she said doubtfully.

"How much longer are you in town?"

Remembering that hour with him in his clean, cold house that was really an art gallery, remembering his reluctance, his chill, how she'd had to wrench every nail of information out of him with a pliers, she felt that nothing had changed. And in the end he might not tell her anything at all.

"Two more days. But I need to know now."

"But I need time to put out feelers."

"Of course you do," she said, looking away to hide her frustration. Mills Lake was giving her damned hard time.

"I'm trying to help, Tillie."

"Really, Adam? Then please *do*."

"And what is it I must do?"

"For starters let Nathan Ely photograph one or two of your Hoyts tomorrow. He's a respected local photographer, *Art World's* hired him. And my article will be dust without photographs. Nathan

91

and I have an appointment at Hoyt's tomorrow morning. What I'm saying is, *the artist himself is welcoming photographs of his work*."

"He's welcoming photographs of what's in his studio. But again, I'm afraid any photography of *my* Hoyts is out."

Recklessly she hoisted her Old Fashioned with both hands and chugged. By the time she set it down, she was feeling warm and quite clever. For instance. What if there were some sinister reason for both Smitty Barker and Quick refusing to allow their Hoyts to be photographed? What if they'd stolen them? What if they'd cheated him on price and didn't want it known? *What if something in the paintings incriminated them—or someone they knew*?

She was jotting notes again when the door opened on a blast of cold air and a man entered. Saluting Helen, he headed for a seat where the bar curved away into privacy and took possession as though it belonged to him. When he threw back his parka hood, she recognized Wilk Steeves. Her heart did an odd little dance.

"Thought you'd be scared off by the storm." Helen, always audible, to her new customer.

"You know these weather cats, Helen," he said. "Drama queens, all of 'em."

She jerked a thumb over her shoulder. "TV says six to eight before midnight."

"Like I was saying."

She wanted to slip off her bar stool and go speak to him, though she didn't know why. At the same time she realized she might be in trouble. Here she was, in a strange Wisconsin bar, one possible murderer picking up her check, another staring at her over his glass. Could it get any worse than this?

She giggled. Or better!

"I really need to go, Professor Quick."

"Adam, remember? And you've barely touched your fries. More to the point, I haven't finished my burger. This was supposed to be a leisurely lunch."

"I know and I'm sorry, but I have another appointment. Thank you for—a memorable experience." Slipping off her stool, hitching her briefcase over her shoulder, she started for the door.

Quick was at her heels. As she passed the exit and rounded the bar toward where Steeves sat chatting up Helen, Quick's hand on her shoulder spun her round.

"This is the way out. Coming?"

"In a minute, Adam."

His eyes knifed between her and Steeves.

"I'll warm up the car," he said evenly, though she thought she heard a warning in his voice.

"So, Matilda," said Steeves as the door closed behind Quick.

"So, City Manager."

He tugged her sleeve and she moved closer.

"Just a word of warning. To a New Yorker like you, Mills Lake must seem like Eden before the fall."

"Um, not precisely."

"Well, trust me: it isn't. Be careful, Tillie."

CHAPTER NINETEEN

By now Nathan Ely was nine minutes late, Tillie checking her watch every other minute as her toes in fashion boots turned rapidly to ice. A car cruised by and she waved, but it kept on going. She was cursing his tardiness when the same car shot back into view and parked. A driver exited only to disappear into the hatchback. Slamming it down, he trudged up the drive toting a load of equipment.

"Is this the place?"

Between the black wool cap pulled low on his forehead and a blacker beard, she saw eyes that hadn't yet said good morning to the day.

"Matilda Roth Hamilton," she said, automatically extending her hand. "And you must be Mr. Ely?"

"Nathan's the name."

"Nice to meet you, Nathan."

"Likewise. You actually from New York?"

"Actually, yes."

"Hoyt's that important?"

"He will be. I'm assuming you know him?"

"Of him, not the same thing."

Tillie's impression of a reclusive Dexter Hoyt was being confirmed hour by hour. "All right then, let's wake him up." She rapped and stepped back from the door.

Silence.

"That looks like a great camera," she said brightly, stamping blocks of ice she remembered as feet. "What kind is it?"

"You know cameras?"

"Um, not exactly." Even in the cold she felt herself blush. "Mine's a point-and-shoot Canon."

Ely curled his lip. "*This* is a Rolleiflex 3.5 TLR—the same model Diane Arbus used. You've heard of her?"

Six years after Arbus's suicide in 1972, Tillie had written an article for *Art World* on an exhibit of Arbus's work. "Of course I have," she said indignantly and saw herself go up a notch in his estimation.

"Here." Ely transferred his tripod into her arms. "Let me have a go at that door." He gave it a shove and it opened soundlessly.

"He sleeps late," explained Tillie as she led the way into the entrance piled with with jackets, boots, scarves and picture frames frosted with drifts of advertisements and unopened mail. Beyond, Hoyt's studio loomed, dark and cavernous.

"Ahoy, Hoyt!" she called. "Tillie here."

"Take a look at this place!" marveled Ely. "I *adore* photographing chaos."

"Hoyt's paintings are the opposite of chaos. Wait until you see them."

"*If* I ever do."

In the studio proper: "Well, how about this one." She pointed to "Lady with Snake" still on its easel, still exuding the brushstroke genius and enigmatic charm that had bowled her over that first day.

"*Cool*!" He raised his camera.

"Not without permission!"croaked Tillie, darting forward to block the painting if necessary. "He must still be in bed. Let me look."

Then she forgot about snakes and ladies.

Beyond the easel hulked the broken-down velour sofa where she'd perched that first day frantically taking notes, trying to get the artist to open up about his paintings and his life, trying to figure out what kind of a man she was dealing with. Now, drawn to it, she looked over the back and saw a pair of red and tan argyle socks that encased two feet. One of the socks had a large hole; out of that hole stuck a grubby toe. As usual, Hoyt was sleeping off a night of painting.

"He's here," she called softly to Nathan. "Should I wake him?"

"I strongly suggest it."

She came round the couch.

Hoyt's hands were tucked under his left cheek. His lips wore a half-smile, his black hair spilled over his forehead, the silver streak

95

strangely luminescent. Playfully she prodded his shoulder, then snatched back her hand.

"Oh, no!" she cried, retreating as though afraid she might wake him from a dream with which she had no business interfering. She forced herself to look at the artist again. Nothing had changed, there was no news of him. Death had drained room and man and left them empty. So that's what death is, thought Tillie: the total absence of color. Of space and of light.

"We have to call the police," she said, finding her voice.

*****

Flashing badges, they announced themselves as Sergeants Crosby and Moss. Tillie couldn't take her eyes off their equipment— leather belts, guns in holsters keeping company with handcuffs, batons, mace cans, walkie-talkies, stun-guns, whistles. She hadn't realized before the formidable armor of the law. Was the world really so unruly?

Crosby whipped out a notebook. "State your business here," he said woodenly. Yet his face struck her as so openly honest that she warmed to him on sight.

"We had an appointment with Mr. Hoyt at ten. Right, Nathan?"

"Right," he said, still throwing looks over his shoulder, itching to photograph the whole scene. She couldn't blame him: he was a professional after all.

"Full names, please," said Moss.

"John Nathan Ely."

"And you?"

"Matilda Roth Hamilton." This time she didn't offer her hand.

"What's your business here?"

"We had an appointment with Dexter Hoyt at ten. I should explain. I've flown in from New York to do a commissioned article about him for *Art World* magazine. Yesterday I reminded Mr. Hoyt that I and a photographer would be here at ten. When we got here, we knocked several times, then when he didn't answer we tried the door. Oddly enough, it was open, so we came in. He was expecting us."

Sergeant Moss, chiseled arrowhead face, raised plucked eyebrows. "Sure about that?"

"Of course I'm sure!" Was Sergeant Moss going to be trouble?

Crosby, though, had focused on Ely. "I think I know you, sir," he said, respect in his voice. "Wasn't it you that took that very fine photograph of my mother and father for their fiftieth wedding anniversary?"

"Are your parents Jim and Rose Mary Crosby?"

"That's right."

"Sure, I remember photographing them. A couple of years ago, wasn't it? They were a pleasure to work with."

Nothing beats local connections, mourned Tillie.

Wading though clutter, Crosby and Moss plowed into the studio where they assembled at the sofa and stood looking down at the body. Moss went through the motions of checking a pulse.

"Call the funeral home, Moss," said Crosby.

Moss detached the radio from her belt. "I'd say the coroner first."

"You think?"

"Youngish healthy-looking male? I think."

"Then we need Forensics."

"They gotta come from Madison, don't they? We can handle the basics ourselves. I'll get evidence bags from the squad."

"Hold it there, Moss. Before we do anything, we notify the Chief."

Nathan ostentatiously slung his camera case over his shoulder, picked up his tripod. "Sorry, guys, I gotta split. I have a photo shoot at eleven."

"Uh-uh," said Moss, nipping round Crosby and blocking Ely's exit. She caressed the pair of handcuffs hanging from her belt. "Right now nobody's going anywhere. Seeing you're both suspects in a case of possible murder."

CHAPTER TWENTY

Maureen Sherpinski reached for her coffee as she turned the pages. Nothing in the forensics report she'd plucked from the fax machine had surprised her thus far except the lengths to which somebody had gone to arrive at what struck her as an obvious conclusion.

No water was found in the stomach of the deceased, a vital sign when a person has fallen into the water alive. Further, no mud, sand, plant fragments under the fingernails or other signs of drowning were dis covered. Forensics also found no water, sand or mud in deceased's air tubes, the presence of which also signals drowning. Nor had the lungs increased in size, another indicator. Lastly, we found no presence of froth in the deceased's air tubes, the most characteristic sign of drowning.

Taking into consideration the length of time between death and examination, Madison Police Forensics still concludes that the late Elizabeth Ann Barker who resided at 513 Freeman Street, Mills Lake, WI, was already dead when she went into lake of the same name.

Forensics further estimates that the body of the deceased entered the lake sometime in December of 1979. This calculation is based partly on Wisconsin DNR records stating that said lake did not officially freeze over until January 9, 1980, and partly on the condition of the remains, which suggest the body was in water some sixty days before its discovery on February 2, 1980.

Normally bodies submerged in water bloat with gases that cause them to surface in a matter of two or three days. This appears not to have happened in the case of E. Barker, suggesting that her body had been weighted down in some fashion. No weight was found by our forensic team, however, perhaps not surprising since the body had been severed into three distinct parts.

The Chief released breath she realized she'd been holding for minutes, or was it years. She'd hoped Ice Lady would go down as a simple case of drowning. Liz Barker swimming out too far. Non-swimmer Liz tipping over a canoe. Liz Barker venturing on thin ice to walk her dog . . . .

But then, why hadn't her disappearance been immediately reported?

She made a third trip to the coffee machine, smiling as she recalled actually spitting out the house brew on her first day at MLPD. Funny what you could get used to.

Moss stuck her head through the door. "A Marilyn Price to see you, Chief." She lowered her voice. "I tried to keep her off your back but she wants the big—"

"*Marianne* Price, please." A tall, dark-haired woman pushed past Sergeant Moss, filling the room with an expensive, spicy perfume. "Your Sergeant said you needed my analysis in a hurry, so here it is."

Still focused on the forensic report, Sherpinski blanked, then realized this must be the hand-writing expert. "I appreciate that," she said, nodding to the only chair and opening the red folder Price handed her. After a few moments she looked up. "You've concluded the letter in question's a forgery?"

"Definitely. Quite an amateur forgery, actually."

"May I ask what your experience is as a handwriting analyst?"

Marianne Price tossed her head. "I've had twenty years litigation experience with a Wisconsin firm I don't choose to name.

Currently I'm retired, though I do private requests, seminars, that sort of thing. This sister in Fort Meyers—"

"Cynthia Easton."

She tapped Sherpinski's desk with a blood-red fingernail. "I don't know her, but I assume the letter was forged so there'd be no questions asked about why Liz wasn't paying her annual visit?"

"I really can't comment about a case in progress."

"Can't you really? I'm very discreet."

To Sherpinski's relief, the fax coughed and began churning out a page. She rose.

"If you'll see Sergeant Moss, she'll handle your payment."

Heavy gold earring clanked as Price tossed her head; again Sherpinski was engulfed by perfume. "No need," she said loftily. "My work is a small contribution to your fight against crime."

"Very much appreciated." Sherpinski retrieved the fax, wondering why she was more irritated by Price's charity than grateful.

She was digesting technicalities when the phone sang.

"Yo, Crosby, what's up?"

Crosby made urgent sounds; she rode over him.

"Look, there's Ice Lady stuff breaking down here right now. Also Mata Hari was just in my face demanding to see you about the letters. Mata Hari? The World War I spy—where's your history? Aka Marianne Price. Yes, I hear you: somebody named Dexter Hoyt's dead. Get Doctor Kazi on it and tell him to file a MLPD medical report. Later, Crosby, later."

100

CHAPTER TWENTY ONE

Since Waterhouse was closed, Tillie could think of nowhere to perch but Bill & Helen's. Ever since she'd discovered the body of the artist she (still) idolized, she'd felt frozen, suspended like a fish in ice, unable to send signals to the outside world. With Moss's declaring that both she and Ely were suspects, she'd fallen into a deeper freeze, a deeper trance.

Vaguely she remembered Sergeant Crosby taking her statement, muttering under his breath because his ballpoint kept quitting; even more vaguely remembered an aristocratic-looking Indian doctor arriving to bend over the body and do whatever doctors do with corpses in police presence. When she and Ely finally had been let go, she'd hiked back to the Manse and instantly phoned *Art World* collect.

"Mr. Jesko? This is Tillie. Yes, still in Wisconsin. There's been a tragedy. You won't believe it, but Dexter Hoyt is dead and the police are calling it murder."

"Inconvenient." Jesko's smoker's voice rasped over the line. "I don't suppose you killed him?"

"Oh, please! I discovered his body, though, and I'm still in shock. Anyway, what now? What happens to my beautiful article, Mr. Jesko?"

"Panic not, Tillie. In my opinion, your article just got a lot more beautiful—gorgeous, in fact. Now we go with 'Genius Murdered, *Art World* reporter held as suspect.' It'll sell five thousand copies."

Even at noon Bill & Helen's was cave-dark, a scattering of regulars hanging upside down in the recesses like bats. Well, not actually hanging upside down of course, but that was her impression. To her surprise Helen waved; she hadn't expect to be recognized. The co-owner was wearing the same green and gold Packers sweatshirt and toting what looked like the same bottle of beer. There was a feeling of eternity about this place.

101

"What'll it be, Tillie?"

Helen's remembering her name lit a small flame of warmth under the ice block. "A coke, please, Helen. And I guess I'd better eat lunch."

"That'll be burger and fries or ribs and fries."

"Just fries," sighed Tillie. "And cole slaw, please."

She pulled out the notebook to jot down the gist of the New York conversation before she forgot it—not that she was likely to. Kathryn Meadows had rung back to say Jesko was coughing up $1,500 for her murdered genius article, a price raise of five hundred dollars. Provided, that is, she put it in his hands in three days. "He won't negotiate the time thing, Tillie. You know our deadlines and you have to admit he's given you a lot of rope."

"Can do," said Tillie falsely. This meant she'd have to write a draft, catch a plane and deliver her article in person to *Art World*'s premises at 537 West Sixth as soon as her plane landed. No, hold on—that was totally unrealistic. She'd have to finish her draft and locate a fax machine in Mills Lake. But what about photographs?

She sipped her coke then, feeling restless and on edge, slid off her bar stool and headed for the juke box crouched in one of the caves next to the pin ball machine. The menu offered a choice of songs she'd either never heard of or heard *ad nauseum*.

"It works." Helen at her shoulder.

"How much?"

"On the house. Nobody plays it, too busy listening to themselves talk or yelling for the Pack."

Barry Manilow, Neil Diamond, Andy Gibbs, Donna Summer. Hesitating between the Bee Gees' "How Can You Mend a Broken Heart" and Waylon Jennings' "The Only Daddy That'll Walk the Line," she punched instead Roberta Flack's "Killing Me Softly," and didn't realize until she was back at the bar how inappropriate, under the circumstances, her choice had been. Yet when Flack had sung the last "with his song," she went back and played it again.

She was jotting in her notebook when the door opened. Like the regulars, she looked up as Wilk Steeves walked in and headed for his usual spot. Impulsively she shot up her hand, then pulled it down; she had no excuse to catch his attention. Not that she wanted to. She could not forget that morning walk with Gigi, never forget his words—incriminating words—drifting to her through fog-white trees.

She would have liked to hear the Flack once more; but that meant passing him and stopping to chat, and she didn't feel like chat. Never the twain shall meet, she murmured, dismissing him and underlining "Fax article tomorrow!" in her notebook three times.

"We meet again."

Wilk stood at her side.

"Let me get that for you." He disappeared and came up with the pen she'd dropped. "Mind if I sit down?"

"No, of course not. How are you?" (Inane, inane!)

He tilted his head, considering. "Pretty well," he concluded. "Yourself?"

"Awful, if you want to know."

He set down his Coke next to hers. "I do want to know. Tell me."

To her horror, she felt tears scalding her eyes. Scrabbling for Kleenex, she blew her nose and took a deep, ragged breath. "Dexter Hoyt is dead. My undiscovered genius. I found him this morning."

He gave her shoulder an awkward pat. "I know," he said. "And I'm sorry."

She raised her head to stare and suddenly she was furious. "Why do you know *everything* always!" she blazed. "And I don't believe for a minute you're sorry!"

He shot her a startled glance. But he didn't leave, as she expected he would. Instead he threw back his head and examined the 1920s tin ceiling, drumming his fingers on the counter, weighing her question.

"I guess I know things, Tillie, because people *expect* me to know every damn last thing that goes down in this town. Excuse me." He signaled Helen, who lumbered over.

"Missus Bill, I've lost a plate of lunch somewhere and I'm starving. Know where I left it?"

She rolled her eyes. "Now tracking your lunch is my job? And by the way, the name's Helen."

He blew her a kiss. When he turned back to Tillie she seemed to have calmed down. He noticed for the first time that she was wearing earrings—silver, with little red enamel hearts in their centers. Old-fashioned they looked. At the same time, he remembered it was Valentine's Day—or perhaps Valentine's Day had been yesterday or the day before? He'd had no call to remember the holiday for years.

"Happy Valentine's day."

"Pardon?"

He reached out and touched one of the tiny red hearts with his fingertip. It trembled. "You're wearing your heart in your ears."

Hands flying to the earrings, she blushed as though caught in a crime. She'd forgotten to wear them on Valentine's Day so had put them on now, liking the way their garnet-red clashed with her rusty hair. Had Wilk Stevens been the sender of that Valentine card? She'd been wondering who her admirer was ever since she opened it. Adam Quick? Even more unlikely, Dexter Hoyt?

"They're pretty."

"Thank you. They belonged to my Ohio grandmother."

"As for being sorry for Dexter's death, maybe I am." He again contemplated the ceiling. "If only because it completes Matilda Roth Hamilton's mission in Mills Lake."

"But you're not sorry for an extraordinary talent cut short?"

Probing his glass with the straw, he noisily sucked up the last drop of Coke. "That's a pretty abstract concept, isn't it—extraordinary talent? If you mean, will I miss running into Dexter Hoyt around town, frankly, no."

"You know I don't mean that! I mean, are you sorry that a remarkable artist is dead?"

"Somehow, not really." He felt rather than saw her recoil. "Though please don't get me wrong. I highly respect your commitment."

Helen slung down two plates. "Yours is hot, Miss Tillie, don't scorch yer fingers."

She stared hopelessly at the steaming fries, thinking of the subtle savory quiches at her favorite Fifty-Fifth and Broadway bistro.

"Nourishment is imperative in situations like this. Eat up." Steeves corralled the catsup from one of the condiment caddies punctuating the counter like oases. "You?"

"No, thanks."

"Fries without catsup? Infidel!" He seized a bunch of fries, stabbed them into a thick red pool, swallowed them in one bite.

"Back to what we were saying," said Tillie, determined to ignore his disgusting orgy of fat, salt and sugar. "Of course it's commendable that you believe in art, whether you understand it or not, as you said. But don't you admit—and I'm not just talking Mills Lake, could be any place—that people fear and hate genius? They may pay it lip service but they hunt it to kill. Because genius shames mediocrity—"

Once more he studied the ceiling as if in search of inspiration.

"I don't know, Tillie. All I can say is that, as far as I know, I'm not afraid of genius. You're going to hate this, but could be I'm not afraid of it because I've never met it."

She looked at him and decided she'd been terribly mistaken. He wasn't handsome after all, bathed in grease, grinning at her with a catsup smear on his upper lip. He had disappointed her: he refused to talk about serious things; he was a clown.

She returned to her own trauma.

"I'll bet you don't know this, Mr. Steeves. The police were actually ready to charge Nathan Ely and me with murder."

"But I do know. They let you both go. Under suspicion, of course."

"Is there *anything* you don't know!" She was furious all over again.

He flung up his hands in protest. "Back off, Tillie. We've already walked this road. Try taking a geographical perspective."

"I don't know what you mean."

"If you consider the whole United States of America, you'll realize I know next to nothing about anything. And if you consider the world—"

"Phone for you." Helen again. This time she delivered two Guest Checks. Tillie reached for her wallet. Crazy, she thought, not for the first time: the very definition of "guest" is they don't pay.

Steeves had disappeared into one of the bat caves. Everything important in town, she decided, must transpire in those caves: the secrets, the wheeling-dealing, the assignations. With sudden longing for her Ferry Manse four-poster, she gathered her equipment.

He returned, struggling into his parka. "Sorry—"

"Let me guess. A sewer's frozen. The asphalt's buckled. A municipal worker's sprained his thumb—"

He leaned in so close she thought he might harm her. "Just shut up, will you! *Why are you so against* me? I can't tell you this, but I'm going to anyway because you don't give a damn and I need to tell somebody. Smitty Barker's in the Jefferson County Jail for murdering his wife."

CHAPTER TWENTY TWO

"Mrs. Klein?"

"Hello? Please speak up."

The voice notched a fraction.

"This is Diane and it's my afternoon at the Clinic. A while ago two policemen came in. I was scrubbing the reception room floor but after they barged in I had to lay down two rolls of paper towels so their wet boots wouldn't track. I heard them ask to see Dr. Barker."

"Diane, you may be the best cleaning woman in Jefferson County but can you please get to the point?"

"Right. Claire told them Dr. Barker was with a client but they said, 'Inform him we're here.' He came out of an exam room and the police took him aside. He shook his head at first but then went into his office and came out wearing his lumberjack shirt, you know the one, and they escorted him out the door. I thought you should know."

"Thank you, Diane. I appreciate your calling."

For Nora the afternoon flowed by like a swift river. Automatically she let Gigi outside, checked the fridge for leftovers in which she had no interest, found her way to the solarium where she sank into a chair and rocked, staring at the frozen lake, the tang of winter geraniums harsh in her nose. Listened for the phone, watched the sun drop down the sky.

When the doorbell rang she froze; then realized it might be news of Smitty and hurried to the front door. Through the glass she saw a mass of red hair and a cold-pinched face with a small red nose. She flinched, then felt herself sinking into a terrible weariness. Matilda Roth Hamilton, New York snoop and the last person on earth she wanted to see. But she shot the bolt.

The beautiful face was crumpled, tears bouncing down its cheeks. In rushed Tillie and grabbed Nora's hands.

"Nora, Nora, I'm so sorry!"

107

"I'm sure you are," said Nora, disengaging firmly.

"You know, then."

"Know what? Please enlighten me"

Tillie recoiled. She'd come to sympathize, not to break news. Wilk Steeves had only confided in her because she "didn't give a damn," but she did. Stalling, she scraped her boots on the mat, heard Gigi barking in some far-away room. Finally she met Nora's eye.

"It's about your friend, Dr. Barker."

Nora lifted her chin. "You're here to tell me something about Smitty I don't know?"

Arrogant, just as she'd been at their first meeting. Cold, superior. After all, Nora Klein might deserve to hear the worst.

"Maybe. Do you know he's been charged with murdering his wife and is in the Jefferson County jail?"

Of all the scenarios Tillie had imagined hurrying along the lake road to break the news, she had not imagined this. Head thrown back, Nora was laughing. Tillie recoiled.

"And here I thought you'd come to walk Gigi," gasped Nora, trying to recover herself. "Well, you *do* walk Gigi, don't you. I didn't suspect you were carrying a sledgehammer up your sleeve."

"Nora—"

"Yes, a sledgehammer. I think you've always wanted to brain me—" She went off into another cascade of laughter. Finally she took a deep breath and shook herself like a dog coming out of water. "Sorry, Ms. Hamilton, I'm reacting badly. Come in and tell me about it."

In the hot and blooming solarium, Nora indicated a lounge chair and Tillie sank into it, immediately feeling luxurious, disoriented and terribly sleepy. Her coat slipped from her shoulders, she let it fall onto the black and white harlequin tiles.

Nora leaned forward. "Frankly, I'm incredulous. How can you possibly know Smitty's been charged?"

Tillie attempted to sit upright, failed. "Because I happened to be with the City Manager when he got the call."

"*You* are chummy with the City Manager?"

Again the disbelief. Tillie might have been insulted except that she herself felt how improbable it was she knew Steeves. "I've been interviewing him for my article. You know—local facts, local color, local lore."

"Oh, yes, the famous article." Nora ripped a geranium blossom from a nearby plant, inhaled and tossed the already-dying blossom away. "God, I loathe the smell of geraniums! *Why* do I bring them in every fall." She turned her chair toward Tillie. "So Wilk actually told you what his call was about?"

"Well, yes. Because he had to suddenly excuse himself."

"Let me get this straight. Our City Manager gets a critical *private* call from the police, then turns round and confides what he heard to a total stranger from New York? That's as bizarre as you coming to inform me what's happened to my closest friend."

"I'm sorry. I didn't mean to intrude, it just happened."

"You've been here what—four days?"

"Five tomorrow."

"And five days gives you the right to rule Mills Lake?"

Now fully awake, Tillie levered herself out of the chair.

"Wait a minute, Nora. What do you mean *rule Mills Lake*? You're calling it all wrong. This is a classic case of blaming the messenger. By sheer chance I heard about Dr. Barker and came to offer you my sympathy." She picked up her coat and briefcase. "Obviously, I made a mistake."

"You're dead right about that."

On the threshold of the solarium, Tillie stopped. "And now you're going to hate me even more. Because I have more bad news you might not know about."

"Jimmy Carter's died of being too good to be true?"

"Dexter Hoyt is dead."

Without a word, Nora got up and pushed past her, leaving Tillie no choice but to trail her through the now-dark house to the front door. (Where was darling Gigi?)

"I'm sorry, Nora."

"No, you're not, you love this. Because you don't *know* Smitty, you don't *know* Dexter, you're just feeding off them for glory and money. Ever heard of the Black Plague? You're it, Matilda Roth Hamilton. So a word of advice from someone who's been here rather longer than five days. Back off."

"Right."

"One more thing, child. You're being played by Wilk Steeves like a trout on a line. If you don't know that, you're a goddamn fool."

CHAPTER TWENTY THREE

The fool burrowed her chin into the fur collar against the wind. It took her three snowy blocks to recover from the war she'd fought with Nora. Because it had been war, all right.

Yet almost always she thought on target, and her target now was getting photographs of Hoyt's paintings she could fax tomorrow with her article to *Art World*.

She'd thought of slipping into Hoyt's studio with Nathan Ely, but the yellow police tape looping the carriage house discouraged that plan. Jailed, Dr. Barker could not give her permission to photograph his Hoyts; would not anyway. One possible source remained.

She was raising her fist to knock at his very secure door when she saw the Pinto pull into the drive and disappear into the garage. Adam Quick emerged carrying a briefcase. He spotted her immediately in the snowy February dusk, signaled her to wait. Eventually he unbarred his front door.

"I know this is unexpected, but may I come in?"

"You may."

"Professor Quick—Adam, I mean—"

"Promising, that. Why don't you shed the coat?"

"I can't stay long," she said, following him into his living room-gallery.

Hoyt's paintings still glowed like jewels against the stark-white walls. Yet for Tillie they now were muted by the artist's death. Irretrievably? She hoped not.

"May I?" She nodded in their direction.

"Worship if you must."

Yet as she moved along the Hoyts, she found she could no longer rejoice in the della Robia blues, clay pinks, tomato reds and rich golds that lent his paintings the texture and spirit of medieval art. She felt instead as though she'd joined a funeral procession. Her favorite saying—*ars longa, vita brevis*— suddenly seemed terribly apt.

"I've a nice chardonnay if you're in the mood."

She turned and realized Quick had been watching her. Immediately she felt uncomfortable. Had he remembered her trying to order the wine at Bill & Helen's and bought a consolation bottle in case she dropped by?

"No, thank you, but please go ahead."

"I will." He left and returned with a bottle and a corkscrew that meant serious business. "You're sure?"

"I'm sure." She watched him extract the cork, then screw a funnel into the neck of the bottle.

"What's that?" Anything to postpone her mission.

"An aerator, of course," he said, and fastidiously poured.

"Actually, I have some bad news."

"Really?" He looked up. "You don't *look* bad news-ish, you know. You look—I don't know—hair of flame and fightin' ready for anything."

What a strange man.

"You know about Dex, of course?"

But the second the words were out of her mouth, she knew he did not. She would have to go through the whole thing again.

"I know he's having a Chicago art show which, as you so pointedly informed me, is ancient news to you."

She'd retrieved her briefcase: her talisman, her only certainty. Now she clutched it tighter, gathering to herself what little she felt she'd accomplished.

"Dexter Hoyt is dead."

Wine splashed from Quick's glass onto the coffee table.

"You jest."

"How could I possibly joke about a thing like that?"

"I don't know, some people find death rather funny. See Joyce's *Finnegan's Wake*. He called funerals *funforalls*."

She leaned forward, appealing to him, trying to steer the conversation back to business. "Actually, Adam, I was the one who found him this morning. Or rather, Nathan and I."

"Nathan?"

"Nathan Ely, the local photographer who's collaborating with me on this article."

"Incredible."

She didn't understand what he found incredible: Hoyt's death or the fact that she and Ely found the body.

"That's all you have to say?"

"That"— Quick fastidiously folded and refolded his handkerchief to blot the wine spill "—and whodunit?"

Tillie sat up straight in the uncomfortable modern state-of-the-art chair. "You think he was murdered?"

Quick splashed more wine into his glass. "Don't you?"

"Maybe," she said cautiously.

" Let me explain." He jumped up to pace the wall of Hoyt's paintings. "I want to be honest. Dex and I had very little in common besides our preference for his art. And, oddly, the fact we both happened to be health fanatics. We debated the subject endlessly. I prefer a traditional doctor, when I can find a good one. Dex swore by the teachings of some holistic guru named Lester Gollanz. You may have noticed Gollanz's well-thumbed tomb lying around his studio? I dismissed Gollanz's voodoo as trash for the credulous. But last fall when I dragged Dex into Madison to see my doctor about a stubborn cold I thought could turn into pneumonia, my traditional Dr. Ciske pronounced him freakishly healthy. That's a long answer to your question. But yes, I doubt Dex died of natural causes."

"Then—"

"Then who killed him? Haven't a clue, though I'm sure to be the chief suspect. Weird professor, divorced. Lives alone, not a churchie, cycles not golfs for exercise, doesn't belong to Rotary or the Legion, hasn't a close friend in town." He rubbed his wrists. "I can feel the cuffs already."

Tillie found nothing to say until she remembered why she was there. She stood up purposefully.

"I don't believe for a minute you're a suspect, Adam. Police don't arrest distinguished university professors. But besides wanting to condole with you about Dexter, I have a favor to ask. You see, my editor's laid down the law: no photographs, no article, no payment. I *need* that money, Adam—though it's not just the money that's at stake but my whole career. *Please* will you let Nathan photograph two or three of your Hoyts? You're my last hope."

"What a racket you're making. Please desist."

Tillie looked at him hard as he stood there scowling—arms scissored across his chest, fists thrust deep in his armpits—and saw it was hopeless. She picked up her briefcase and turned to go. She'd reached the door when he finally spoke.

"All right, all right. Damn it, Tillie, I don't like it but I do realize that *Art World* needs photographs."

She ran to him and seized his hands. They were like ice.

"Thank you, thank you. May I call Ely right now?"

"The phone's in the kitchen."

His immaculate kitchen hummed softly with appliances she doubted produced the comforts they were intended for. But when she saw the wall-model phone in harvest gold with its twisty six-foot cord, she smiled. Her Ohio grandparents' very phone, though in their kitchen it was part of a nineteen-sixties harvest-gold and avocado scheme. Its very existence on his wall made her nuclear physicist seem more human.

Ely answered on the third ring. She reported, asked him to hold, ran back to Quick in the gallery.

"He can do it today. Tomorrow he can't."

"Today?" Quick checked his watch. "It's going on five."

Through a window Tillie saw that it was already dark. "I'm sorry but it's his only time."

"All right." He smiled. "Have it your way, but right now I need to unwind, eat, catch the news."

"Understood. Some time very soon, though, I want to hear about that rich-rich patron."

Quick looked away. "I'm afraid that was another minor sin," he said finally. "This time of addition, not omission. You were so

114

let down when I told you about Dex's Chicago show—well, perhaps I, ah, improvised." He raised sharp shoulders in a shrug.

"You *made up* that rich-rich patron?"

But Quick had recovered. "Come back with your photographer at seven. That's my final offer."

CHAPTER TWENTY FOUR

"Do you know Adam Quick?"

She'd persuaded Ely to pick her up at the Manse where, waiting for him, she'd made deep inroads into the cache of raisons, pumpkin seeds and chocolate she'd stowed in her suitcase for emergencies. And she had actually penned—she loved that archaic word—five more pages of The Article.

"Not to my knowledge."

"I thought you might. Being a photographer, you must meet lots of people."

"Yes. Graduates, brides, and folks celebrating being shackled fifty years."

"That would not be Professor Quick."

"I'd guessed it wouldn't. This must be the house."

She always thought of Quick's house as figuratively dark, but now it was dark literally, only a 40-watt bulb over the side door illuminating the premises. The gate still bore the sign 24/7SECUR, the walk was already drifted with snow. Snow, so constant since she'd arrived in Wisconsin that this time she hadn't noticed it was falling.

"Doesn't look like your professor's at home."

"He must be, he said seven o'clock."

"So what now?"

"We knock."

Ely locked his Mazda, trailed her up the walk. She rang the bell three times, knocked, finally pounded with both fists. They waited, snow silting their shoulders.

She turned to Ely. "Hopeless," she said.

Quick had given her the slip, the brush-off, the finger. He'd said he'd let Ely photograph his Hoyts when he knew he wouldn't. He was inside, but he didn't intend to answer the door. Was he punishing her for having caught him in a lie? In any case, he'd played her for a fool.

Her natural impulse was to fight back, but she no longer had it in her. Adam knew her career was riding on this article, this *illustrated* article. Why hadn't she realized from the beginning that he'd been working against her?

"What now?"

"Nothing, I guess. I guess it's over."

"This sucks." Shoulders touching, they stood on the walk, snow up to their ankles, Tillie staring at the door she realized she'd never really opened.

"Thanks for coming out, Nathan. Sorry it didn't turn out. I can walk back to the Manse."

"But there's got to be other Hoyts I can photograph."

"Not that I know of."

"What about his studio?"

"Well, sure, but the police have sealed it."

"Let's just take a look."

Installed again in his car, she realized he was still wearing the same black knit cap, a disguise completed by the black beard efficiently obscuring the rest of his face. If she had to describe Nathan Ely, she could testify only to black eyes and a rather elegant nose.

"I'm curious," she said, buckling in. "What do you look like in summer when you ditch the knit cap and shave your beard? Is there actually a face under all that?"

"Wanna see?" He yanked off the cap and black curls spilled over his forehead. "That's half anyway. You'll have to wait for summer for the rest."

"I won't be here in summer."

"Your loss, baby, your loss."

She suggested he park down the block from Hoyt's studio. Coolidge was dark, only one or two bright windows and a leaning lamppost that barely lit Hoyt's drive.

"That the place?"

"Right." Suddenly Sue Ellen flashed across her mind. Surely Hoyt's paintings automatically went to his next of kin so perhaps she'd already raided his studio. If so she was truly doomed.

Ely lowered his window and a ridge of snow flopped into his lap. Brushing it off impatiently, he peered across the street. "I don't see any tape."

Spirits recovered, she flashed him a wicked smile. "Let's check it out."

"All my life I've been waiting for a chance to be arrested with you. Not."

"Look at it as a chance to be creatively illegal."

"We'll be seen."

Twisting in her seat, Tillie surveyed the street. "Empty, void, deserted. Look, this was your idea, not mine. Got a flashlight?"

"I'm the sensible type."

"Sensible's good. Come on, Nathan, be a sport."

"Victim, you mean." He got out, rummaged for his equipment, shouldered it and followed her up the drive, head swiveling for witnesses to their crime. Which, he reminded himself, he'd initiated. *Why* had he. After all, he was a local with a lot to lose, whereas Tillie could just hop a plane back to New York.

Except that now it was night, the place looked as it had the day she'd first knocked at Hoyt's door long—no—just days ago. Shabby-chic Victorian boho, dead vines masking small carriage house windows. A secret place, an inviting place. Not Coolidge Street, not Freeman either. A world unto itself.

"Guess we'll have to break in."

A bead of sweat crawled from Ely's cap. "I don't like this."

"*I* love it!"

Incredibly, as it had that first day, the door opened when Tillie turned the knob. She laughed. Five blocks away Adam Quick hard armed himself with a state-of-the-art security system, while the artist he collected was indifferent to protecting his work.

Tillie pulled Ely inside. "Relax, Hoyt owes me this." Running her hand over the wall, she located a light switch.

"Jesus, do you *crave* to be seen? Here, use this."

He passed Tillie his flashlight and immediately she was back in Ohio lying under quilts devouring the Nancy Drew mysteries her mother had treasured until the January night, when she was just seventeen, she'd eloped with Tillie's father, Edward Hamilton.

"This way." Nathan groaned, yet against his will found himself yielding to Tillie's crazy mood of adventure.

"There's a painting I *really* want photographed. It used to be on an easel; yes, it still is. If you can get a good shot of 'Lady with Snake,' Nathan, I'll worship you all the days of my life."

"Not good enough." But his tripod was up and he was affixing the famous Rolodex that Dianne Arbus had used.

"Got it, just remove your face from my photograph."

She retreated and beamed her way across the room to the bank of windows that overlooked the garden of Smitty and Liz. She located a cord and a huge venetian blind clattered down. She sneezed. "Now we can turn on a light."

"Hold it! Those front windows, somebody'll see—"

"Covered in vines. Do relax."

He didn't believe her; yet again, against his will, the excitement of the quest gripped him.

"A couple more and we're out of here. Here's another I absolutely must have."

"Then set it on the easel, will you? I can't photograph it on the floor."

Handling 'Lady with Snake' like a holy relic, she replaced it with her second favorite and shone the flashlight on it. Ely whistled.

"Better than the first."

"I don't agree, but close."

Ely fiddled with lenses until the face of a fox that also seemed to be the face of a woman come into focus. He clicked the Rolo three times.

"Now for number three." She strafed the flashlight up and down the west wall. "That's funny, it was right there, one of the few paintings Hoyt actually hung. A small canvas"— She lifted her shoulders in confusion.

"Pictures are not fixed objects, you know. Probably he took it down."

"Wait." Handing him the flashlight, she headed for a stack of canvasses propped against the sofa that she'd always wanted to explore. "Light, please." Dropping to one knee, she filed through the paintings. "Not here either."

"Maybe he sold it."

"Maybe," she said doubtfully.

"What the hell's going on here?"

A hooded man stepped out of the shadows squinting down the barrel of a rifle aimed between Ely's eyes. They froze.

Heart banging, Tillie was the first to recover.

"Hello," she said in what she hoped was a steadying voice. "I'm Matilda Roth Hamilton from New York. I came to interview Mr. Hoyt for a major article I'm writing about him. This is my photographer, Nathan Ely."

"*Not* her photographer," muttered Ely.

Staring incredulously at her outstretched hand, the man slowly lowered his rifle.

"That doesn't explain what you're doing in Dex's studio. Looks like breaking and entering to me. I'm calling the police." He started for Hoyt's phone on the littered coffee table but Tillie stopped his hand.

"Actually, we don't know what *you're* doing here."

"You don't have to, do you. You're the trespassers."

"But you're trespassing too."

"Dammit, I'm Dex's neighbor. He gave me a dupe key a while ago, asked me to watch his place. *That's* what I'm doing here."

"But his door was open. Why was it, if you're supposed to be watching his place?"

"That's not the question. An open door doesn't give you the right to enter."

"But this does." Locating her briefcase, Tillie unzipped it, pulled out a piece of paper and steered it under his nose. "Give him some light, Nathan."

"What's this?"

"You're looking at a legal document allowing me access to Dexter Hoyt and his paintings." Tillie tapped the page. "See his signature at the bottom? Dexter T. Hoyt." (Why hadn't she asked him what the "T" stood for. Now it was too late.)

"It's simple," said Ely, riding on her bravado as he struggled with camera equipment and flashlight and wished he'd never heard of Matilda Roth Hamilton. "New York wants photographs. That's absolutely all this is about. I take one more shot and we're outta here—"

Tillie shook her rusty mop; drops hit her cheeks: she hadn't realized she'd been sweating fear. "Except," she smiled trustingly at the hooded man, "that I'd love to have your name so I can thank you in print for your assistance."

Shooting off a round of bad words, the man set aside his rifle and threw back his hood. His short-clipped brown hair, high-boned cheeks, and blue eyes did not look sinister. He swiped his runny nose with the back of his hand, then seemed to notice Ely for the first time. He frowned.

"Wait a mo. Aren't you the guy who photographed Icehenge when we were working on it?"

"That's me."

"You have the studio on West Lake?"

"Correct."

"I've always wondered who sent you down there."

"Can't remember who said there was action on the lake, but I thought I'd check it out. So you're the one who designed it?"

"Devon Bond, that's right. With more than a little help from my friends."

"Small world."

"A mutual admiration society," interrupted Tillie, "how nice. Good to meet you, Devon. I hope we've convinced you we aren't burglars? As Nathan says, one more photo and we're gone." Her eyes challenged him.

Bond grabbed his rifle, but its business end hung at his knees.

"It's okay, I guess. "Dex is—was—careless with keys and that lock's so old it doesn't work half the time. I'll wait while you finish up here."

Finally Ely shouldered his equipment and they all headed for the door.

"One more thing, Devon," said Tillie. "This may be private information, but now that Hoyt's dead —"

"—doesn't make it any less private—"

"It does, though, don't you think? Anyway, he told me his sister believes *he* murdered Liz Barker."

"What a bunch of bullshit! Dex wouldn't hurt a mouse."

"Maybe, but it was weighing on his mind."

"What are you suggesting? That he killed himself as a kind of confession?"

"It crossed my mind. But then why is Dr. Barker in jail?"

"Look." Devon out the front door. "I'm a simple man. I keep a key to the carriage house because Dex asked me to. So since his death I've kinda been looking out for the place, felt I owed him as a neighbor. As for who killed who and why, I haven't a clue. All I want is to lock up and hit the sack."

Tillie and Ely tramped down the drive. "Get in, I'll drive you home."

"I was hoping you'd offer. Listen, Nathan. If Devon's the keeper of the keys, why did we find Hoyt's studio wide open?"

"Didn't he say something about old locks? Listen, Tillie, and I quote: I'm a simple man. All I can do is try to get those photos to you tomorrow."

"That's not simple, Nathan: that's heroic."

In her room, Tillie stripped, vowing to find a laundromat soon. Or not, because her mind was buzzing with new information. Devon Bond had a key to Hoyt's studio. There was nothing, therefore, to stop him from purloining (she loved that word) the painting missing tonight on Hoyt's wall. And if he'd removed it, he must have had a reason.

122

She must find out whether he owned a boat, maybe a white sweater.

CHAPTER TWENTY FIVE

"Ted Gage has Hoyt paintings," Smitty had told her the day she'd visited him. How could she have forgotten that vital information until now? She must find Gage without delay.

Entering an old building on East Lake's business block, she was surprised to find she could only access his office by elevator, not associating elevators with Mills Lake. It rose for all of one floor and opened onto an outer room where behind a desk a secretary was tapping up a storm on an electric typewriter. Tillie stating her business, she smiled and aimed a thumb over her shoulder at a closed door. "You're expected," she said, intent again upon the keys.

"You found me."

Ted Gage rose, pressed her hand briefly. He was even taller than she'd remembered. No white turtleneck today, but a grey suit set off by a blue shirt and blue and silver striped tie. He motioned her to a chair. "This is the old Bank of Mills Lake building, you know," he said, as though it was the choicest venue in town.

"I didn't know." Among the gaggle of names on a plaque next to the elevator, however, she'd noted that Ted Gage was next in line for the throne. "I appreciate you seeing me so promptly. I hope you don't mind Barry giving me your number."

He waved away minding Barry, picked up a folder lying in front of him, opened it, closed it, set it aside. "What can I do for you?"

"What you might expect. Dr. Barker told me you own Hoyt paintings. That's exciting and I very much hope you'll let me see them."

He frowned, ran a thumb along his lean jaw, gazed at the ceiling, lowered the frown at her.

"This puts me in an awkward position."

"I'm sorry."

"I suppose you can't help asking about such things, no matter how inconvenient to certain people in town. You're on a paid assignment."

Tillie opened her mouth to apologize, did not. "As you say, I'm on assignment, and my main job is getting to know Hoyt's work." She smiled in what she hoped was a winning way. "I admit I was surprised when Dr. Barker told me you own Hoyts. From our conversation the other night I got the impression you dislike him rather intensely."

"My feelings about Dex are neither here nor there. I just hope Smitty didn't give you the impression I have a large collection. I own only two."

She tried to hide her disappointment. "Still—"

"And those two I only bought to save him from starving."

"Somebody pays Hoyt's bills," Wilk Steeves had told her. How unlikely that that somebody turned out to be Ted Gage.

"May I see them?"

"Are you carrying a camera?"

"No."

"Because I won't allow you to photograph them."

"How familiar that sounds."

He ignored her remark, picked up the folder again. "Give me your word you won't refer to these paintings in your article?"

"Must I?"

"Absolutely."

"If I must, I must—though obviously I'd like nothing better."

"Of course you would. That's why I'm going to ask you to sign an agreement to that effect before we go any further." He opened the folder, slid it across his desk. She stared at a very legal-looking document.

"Then you don't trust my word?"

"Not in the least."

"That's pretty insulting, Mr. Gage."

"Not really, Matilda. You don't live here, you have no loyalty to this place. You'll fly back to New York and New York will take over. And in New York, anything goes." He pressed a buzzer. "Pam," he said into a machine. "I'd like you to witness a signature."

The efficient secretary entered the room and Tillie found herself with a pen in her hand. "I haven't finished reading what I'm supposed to sign," she protested.

"Let her read it, Pam."

"It's perfectly straightforward."

She came to the line waiting for her signature. "And if I won't sign?"

"Then," said Gage with a smile, "I will personally escort you to the door."

Tillie sighed and signed, Gage after her, Pam as witness.

"You know where to file this." The secretary nodded, swept up the folder and quietly closed the door behind her.

Shooting back his chair, Gage peddled across the carpet to a large metal safe Tillie hadn't noticed before. Fiddling the lock, he reached inside, pulled out two canvases and propped them against the safe. He motioned her closer.

Tillie drew a sharp breath.

Liz Barker—again. But this time a naked Liz, head flung back, legs splayed. Liz devoured by the eye of the artist, raped by his brush.

"The same woman he usually paints." She tried to keep her voice neutral and realized she was failing. "But in my opinion these two paintings are excessive, and for me that means they're not art. I don't know what else to say."

"As agreed, you aren't going to say anything."

Suddenly she was quite angry. "Then why show me these paintings at all?"

His grip on her arm was painful as he piloted her toward the door.

"Because you asked me to. And because, Matilda Roth Hamilton, in my view you needed to see them. Why? Because you have a shockingly naive—or is 'uninformed' a better word?—idea of the man you're writing about. And that idea should nots be perpetuated. That's all."

126

CHAPTER TWENTY SIX

Jim Jesko's time limit, conveyed through sub-editor Kathryn, had thoroughly shaken Tillie: she realized her article *must* be delivered tomorrow or scratched. In her room she fanned out her notes on a Victorian dressing table meant for penning a love letter or filing an opalescent nail.

She decided she'd been quite brilliant about "Woman with Snake," adequate about "Woman and Dove." She'd given one of Hoyt's landscapes—dreamscapes, really—a thorough analysis, just because it was so rare for Hoyt to paint something besides a woman. And yes, she'd made the point that he never painted men, as far as she knew.

She clicked her pen against her teeth. Something was nagging her. She got up, set the kettle on the hot plate, tore open a packet of cocoa, emptied it into a delicately-flowered Victorian cup. Waiting for the kettle's whistle, she saw again the missing painting that had hung on Hoyt's studio wall. Black framed, though Hoyt never framed in black; an abstract, though he never painted abstracts. Probably that's why it kept nagging her. Had he sold it? Possibly. Had Devon Bond purloined it (she loved the word) because it incriminated him?

And what about Ted Gage's Hoyts? She'd signed an agreement to say nothing about them, but nothing could stop her from thinking about them intensely. Why did he own them? Buying two paintings would hardly keep Hoyt from "starving" unless he'd paid big money for them. Tillie tried and failed to picture the cautious lawyer parting with thousands for a man he disliked. Maybe Gage was simply addicted to porn, yet porn must be widely available from sources not charging an artist's price? It all came back to Liz Barker again. Interviewing Hoyt was the one reason she'd come to Mills Lake, yet Liz—to her astonishment—had dominated the scene from day one.

Ted Gage, Liz's lover? Why else would he own those paint-ings.

The kettle shrieked and at that moment she knew she was being watched.

CHAPTER TWENTY SEVEN

"Barry!"

She hadn't closed her door, hadn't realized he'd been standing there. Her hand shook as she poured boiling water over the cocoa.

"I'm having a cup," she said needlessly. "Oh, and I need to call Nora. I was just coming to ask if I could use the house phone."

"There's an extension right here in the hall," said Boycks, looking at her curiously.

She joined him and saw a phone she'd never noticed on a table next to her door.

"Want me to ring her?" When she nodded, he dialed, then passed her the receiver.

"Nora?" Her voice sounded unsteady to her ears. "Tillie here. I was hoping I could walk Gigi later this afternoon." She smiled at Boycks, wishing he'd leave.

"Well, I don't know."

"I'd love to, one more time."

"Does that mean you're leaving?"

"I am."

"Really. I thought you'd taken root here."

Root? "Actually my plane leaves early tomorrow morning. About Gigi—"

"You do know, don't you, that you're abnormally attached to my dog?"

"Ultra-abnormally. Say in about an hour?"

"I suppose so. I'm going out but I'll leave the key. You know where."

"Do I?"

"Under the door mat. I believe in originality."

"Thanks, dear Nora."

No thanks in return, but that was Nora. Tillie shrugged and hung up the phone. Boycks had slipped away.

*****

The house was fogged in, the lake a thick white quilt. In case Nora hadn't left, Tillie knocked and was rewarded by a volley of barks. As promised, she found the key under the thick coir mat. Inside, Gigi danced about her, forepaws pressed to her white chest.

"Okay, pup, let's go. But where's your leash?" Busy doing her dance, Gigi didn't answer.

Not on the hook next to the front door. Not on the kitchen counter. Nora should have left the leash in an obvious place, but she hadn't. Tillie shivered. What was wrong with her today? She decided there was something about houses when people who lived in them were gone. She'd felt the same in Hoyt's silent studio after his death, as though he were watching behind a curtain. Now she felt as though Nora was more present than if she were actually at home.

"Come on, Gigi, let's find that leash." But no leash in the dining alcove where Nora had poured coffee that first meeting, nor in the lush solarium smelling of damp earth and winter blossoms. She hesitated, unfamiliar with the rest of the ground floor, until the dancing dog led her to another door. Furtive as a thief, she opened it.

A large formal living room. White brick fireplace, massive low round table waiting to receive cocktails or afternoon tea. Four-foot Chinese vases bursting with dried blue hydrangeas. And, she realized with a jolt, enough paintings to constitute a small museum. Why had Nora claimed she considered painting irrelevant and knew nothing about Hoyt's art!

She began to explore.

American primitives so rare as to be almost unobtainable on the market—well done, Nora. Left of the fireplace—*was that a real Cezanne*? Quite likely, she decided, remembering Nora's "If you ever have the privilege of examining my house you'll discover France is my country of choice." And there, over a bookcase, Corot's "Ville d'Avray." Now *that* had to be a copy because she'd seen the original in the National Gallery last October—or had Nora

130

bought it since! Dizzied by both the money and the impeccable taste on display, Tillie felt nothing was impossible.

Leash forgotten, she sank onto a section of the white leather couch before the fireplace. For the first time since she'd signed on for the Hoyt article, doubt probed a cold finger. Could she *really* compare Hoyt to these masters? And if she couldn't . . .

But Gigi had dashed to the fireplace grate, snatched something out and was shaking it to death on the hearth rug.

Tillie shot from the couch. "Bad girl, give it here!"

Gigi growled low in her throat, then bowed and dropped her find onto the hearth rug. Tillie picked up what appeared to be an angle of frame. To it was attached a singed patch of canvas.

She switched on a lamp and saw the fragment was black, not charred but painted. A bolt of excitement shot through her. Could this possibly be the remains of the abstract that had hung on Hoyt's wall?

When Nora had invited her in for coffee that first morning, she'd thrown off the mink she was wearing and tossed it onto a chair, a gesture burned in Tillie's brain. What then? Had she wrapped herself in something white like a sweater or a shawl? Tillie couldn't remember. She left the room looking for a closet.

A closet in a hallway leading to the kitchen contained a silver mink jacket in a plastic garment bag, a shiny green rain parka, and a long white coat. She touched the soft wool of the coat appreciatively, but this was no shawl.

In Hoyt's painting there had been a dark rectangular shape that might be a boat. Nora lived on the lake; she must own one? Tillie re-found the solarium. Carefully parting the fleshy leaves of a giant Christmas cactus, she found herself staring through glass at a large, tarp-swathed object riding high on a land station. It could only be a boat.

One down, two to go: a white something and a beetle. Had anyone asked her, she could not have explained her now strong hunch that Hoyt's painting referred to Nora. But that's the nature of a hunch, isn't it, she told herself.

131

She became aware of a dog barking, desperate to go out. In the foyer she found Gigi dancing in front of a large chest.

"Gigi, Gigi," said Tillie, "where *is* that damned leash!" As a last chance, she heaved open the chest lid and stared into the contents. Pairs of gloves, bags of ice-melt, pairs of small snowshoes, ice scrapers, birdseed. And lo, a leash. "Smart girl!" she praised, slipping the red harness onto the quivering body.

Outside, fog smoked as though the snow banks themselves were exhaling. Nothing moved in the whiteness. That day, the day she'd met Nora and Smitty, had been cold and clear; she remembered Barker's nostrils smoking like a dragon's. Today she thought she could smell spring round the corner.

Quality-rating each snowbank, Gigi finally squatted to pee.

"Good girl, but it's too late now for a walk."

Inside she checked her watch: past four. She hadn't intended to spend so much time at Nora's. "Got to go, Gigi," she said, scooping up the dog into an apology hug for not giving her a walk. She was at the front door when her own words *"Hiding it"* buzzed like an alarm in her ear.

Switching on the overhead, she heaved open the trunk lid again. Scarves, road salt, birdseed: the same jumble. This time, however, she dove into the trunk to her armpits, pulling out rubber garden boots, yardsticks, trowels, plant food, a KEEP OFF THE GRASS sign. She was about to give up when her fingers closed on something soft and yarny. She brought it up—a diver retrieving shipwreck treasure—and sat back on her heels.

"I hope you had a nice walk."

Nora stood in the hall pulling off her gloves.

Tillie sprang to her feet. "Oh, yes," she heard herself say above her pounding heart, "an excellent walk. Though I had a terrible time finding Gigi's leash."

"The leash is always on the hook right of the door."

"But it wasn't."

"So you looked for it." Nora nodded at the open trunk.

"I had to."

"Of course you did." Nora shrugged off the mink, tossed it aside: the haunting gesture. "You're leaving us tomorrow, you said."

"At dawn."

Nora nodded. "Safe travels. And *merci beaucoup* for walking Gigi, Matilda. She will miss you."

Tillie stood for a moment in the drive looking at the house and behind it the lake rosy as an apricot as the sun slipped behind trees foresting its west side. She turned away. Would she ever see Sue Ellen and Nathan and Barry Boycks and Smitty again? Not likely. She realized with surprise that the thought saddened her.

Up the hill, she paused at Adam Quick's 24/7SECUR gate. Would she miss even the professor? She would not allow herself to: he had been against her from the beginning.

With twilight came cold and the sudden glitter of a star or two; then, incredibly, flakes of snow again began to fall. Tillie clapped on the rabbit-fur earmuffs. She passed the church with its brave "God Is Still Speaking" sign, the fluorescent Mobile station, the handsome Gothic library, the respectable Ionic pillars of the bank. Snow groaned and creaked under her boots, but she'd accomplished what she'd come to do—in most ways. Turning up Mulberry she could see the Manse windows glowing a welcome.

In a sudden swoop of ecstasy, Tillie dropped her briefcase and flung her arms wide, whirling round in the snow to a tune she couldn't get out of her head. "Killing Me Softly," she sang, "with his song—"

Or was the song not in her head at all, but outside and very near? Still she was feeling such happiness that for a split second she thought the blow to her skull was part of her rapture. That rapture ended as she plunged into blackness.

CHAPTER TWENTY EIGHT

"Give me one good reason, Chief, why Doc Barker's currently languishing in the Jefferson County jail!"

Languishing. Where did Moss come up with these words? Had she in her dubious youth been one of those snotty English majors?

"We've gone over this, Moss."

"Not with me you haven't, I don't have a clue."

The Chief plunged a ball-point pen into her hair, inadvertently slashing her scalp blue. Great to have go-go officers on the force, but in the case of Cate Moss one "go" would be plenty.

"Because," she said, not as patiently as she'd have liked, "we've officially charged him for Dexter Hoyt's death. As you know."

"Yes, but on what evidence?"

"Moss, you were at the meeting."

"Was not. You assigned me to the patrol car that day."

She realized Moss was right. "Okay," she said, folding her hands and willing patience. "As for evidence, we've got a handwriting analyst's verdict that the letter from Liz to her sister was a forgery. On a hunch, we managed to round up samples of her husband's writing. This same expert says Doc Barker wrote that letter."

"But—"

Sherpinski sliced her off. "I clearly remember you stating in meeting that whoever forged that letter was the murderer."

"I did. But I said Liz Barker's murderer, *not* Dexter Hoyt's."

"Moss, I hate to keep bustin' your bubble, but I put a rush on Madison and for the first time in living memory their lab bounced right back. They say there was enough pentobarbital in Hoyt to kill a horse, let alone a man."

"Pento—"

"Vets use it to put down big animals." She watched Moss's mouth drop as she processed the information. "And now that you know, what I've just told you goes no further."

Sherpinsky's phone drilled. She picked up, nodded, began jotting. "I'll have an officer there in five." Hanging up, she looked at Moss and knew how badly she wanted to be that officer. Instead she hit the intercom. "Emergency at the Manse," she rapped into the phone. Moss heard a voice crackle on the other end, then the Chief said, "Thanks, Crosby. Might be attempted murder. Go for it."

*****

Crosby toiled up the Manse staircase behind Barry Boycks and into a room dominated by a tall canopied bed. In the middle, like a small fish on a huge platter, lay a young woman. Approaching, he recognized her as the girl he'd found with Nathan Ely in Hoyt's studio after his death. She lay there so still. Only her tangled hair seemed alive, curling like ivy over a pillow as white as her face.

He cleared his throat; women in distress always—well—distressed him. "What's happened here?"

Barry Boycks didn't often get a chance to dramatize.

"I'm in the kitchen making myself an *omelette roulée* (he enjoyed Crosby's blank look) and I hear the front door bang as though the wind blew it open, which it can't since it's solid oak. So I go check and there's Wilk Steeves, our City Manager—"

"I know who Wilk is—"

"—with this girl in his arms. I recognize her, it's Tillie, I mean she's staying here, of course I would. What's going on, Wilk? I ask, and Wilk says, 'I found her in a snowbank a couple of blocks from here, so I grabbed her up and brought her here.'"

Crosby drove his pen furiously. "What time would that be?"

"Six, six-thirty?"

"Then what?"

"I telephoned the EMS, of course. Ambulance came right away and took her to Fort. I don't know what went on there, but Wilk must've stayed because he brought her back here some time after midnight, carried her upstairs and here she is."

A secret romantic, Crosby felt he should light candles or say a prayer for the beautiful red-haired maiden lying so still, white

135

hands folded on the flowers of the quilt. Instead he said harshly: "What's the diagnosis?"

"Hypothermia, is that what they call it? Plus concussion. I don't know what's under that bandage and don't want to know. But apparently Wilk got to her in time."

"So what do you want MLPD to do?"

Boycks flung up his hands as though the point was obvious. "Look, Crosby, *somebody* knocked her out and dumped her into that snowbank, right?"

"Maybe, maybe not. Does she drink?"

Boycks thought of Tillie dutifully swallowing half of his excellent Old Fashioned. "Not to my knowledge."

"Could she have slipped on ice, hit her skull?"

"I wasn't there, was I! Maybe check with Streets to see if there was ice?"

It dawned on Crosby that Boycks was dancing on hot coals. Since the young lady was staying at his inn, he might feel implicated. Suddenly he felt sorry for him. "I'm just trying to get the facts, Barry, no blame to you. What's the prognosis, do you know?"

"Fort Hospital released her, that should be a positive sign." He moved toward the door, inviting Crosby to follow him. "Damn it, this has been no picnic. For sure it's going to reflect badly on this place. How about a quick drink? I've got a bottle of good brandy socked away for an occasion. And this has been an occasion, believe me."

"Thanks, Barry, it's a little early for me." He guessed his refusal might further contribute to Boyck's unease and regretted it. "Give me a raincheck, okay?"

136

CHAPTER TWENTY NINE

Back at police headquarters, Crosby headed down the hall under the buzzing neon lights that tended to bring on one of his headaches. He was sure Sherpinsky had packed it in long ago; he was wrong.

In the break room she was knuckling her eyes as she stared at the record book in front of her. When she looked up, Crosby saw dark shadows under her eyes and felt a pang of sympathy.

"You're back."

"I am." Crosby scraped a chair up to the table, reached for his notes, slid them across the table.

She scanned them swiftly. "So, Crosby." She plucked a pen from a row of soldiers in a vinyl pocket protector, an accessory that had earned her the affectionate nickname Dorkie. "What actually went down?"

Mainly to keep her company, Crosby got up, filled a mug for himself at the coffee machine. "Okay." He set down the mug. "When I got there subject was in bed. She'd been taken to Fort Emergency, examined and released."

"No serious damage then?"

"Concussion, hypothermia. Apparently she was found in time."

"Thank god. Three murders we definitely don't need." She pushed back her chair, folded her arms. "Okay, let me ask you this. What's our City Manager doing out on the streets on a dark snowy evening?"

"I understand he's into jogging, running, that stuff." Why did he feel he must defend Steeves? "For Tillie's sake, it's lucky he is." Yet he'd been wondering the same thing. "Anyway, in my opinion, I think somebody wanted Matilda dead."

She narrowed grey eyes at him. "For real?"

"Maybe it's too soon, but I gotta think—" He ducked his head diffidently.

"Relax. It's my take too, actually. Yet I ask myself, *why*? A young writer from New York in town on a magazine assignment—who'd want to kill her? Who could she possibly threaten?"

Crosby shoved away his untasted black coffee. "At this point it's guesswork, right?"

"Right."

"If you want my guesswork, Chief, I think Matilda Roth Hamilton (he smiled to himself because he knew her whole name) got too close for comfort, as they say, to the subject of her article."

"Hoyt? But why would that put her in danger?" Sick of coffee, Sherpinsky followed Crosby's example but too energetically and her mug shot off the table. Crosby leapt from his chair.

"Sorry, sorry. Too much caffeine, I'm flyin'."

"Understood." He went for the paper towel dispenser, wiped down his pants, had a brief go at the cheap linoleum that had received most of the Chief's offering. "Look, can we run with this? The why, I mean."

"Okay. I don't think this has any connection with Ice Lady, because that happened before MRH came to town. But suppose she knows or suspects who murdered Hoyt?"

"How could she?"

"Not sure, but I think that's our line of investigation. Who else would attack her and dump her in a snowbank but somebody who's afraid of her knowledge?"

"At least he didn't murder her—"

"That's probably accidental. Acute hypothermia could have killed her. Or the blow to her head." Sherpinski chewed the end of that abused pen. "It was damn cold out. Our potential murderer must have counted on that."

"Don't we have to think about one of the local sex offenders?"

"Those at the Mill Hotel? What would be the motive? Anyway, we keep them under pretty close observation."

"I didn't know that."

"Welcome to the lower depths."

Lower depths? Crosby liked it, it had a kind of ring.

138

"Back to last night. Steeves comes along by chance, finds the girl, carries her to the Manse. She survives—suffering only mild hypothermia."

"And concussion. But, yeah, that's the way it looks."

Sherpinski arched her eyebrows.

"But do you really think, Crosby," she said, tossing the pen at him and missing, "that Wilk's finding her was by chance?"

CHAPTER THIRTY

Tillie searched for a fax machine, her briefcase heavy as a bowling ball. She wandered through a mall stories high and miles long; she passed a boutique selling leashes, a store peddling swimsuits and snowshoes, an official-looking building with a creek running through it, a bar with a hundred jukeboxes. She ran back and forth and up and down until, at the end of a long hall, she saw a blinking red FAX sign. She pulled out her article but when she got to the Fax she saw it was a set of instructions about building a boat. With a gasp of fear, she sat bolt upright to discover she was deep in quilts in the four-poster. Light filtering through white curtains hurt her eyes, her head ached.

She also discovered she was not alone.

"Barry let me in, I hope you don't mind."

Tillie stared at the person sitting three feet from her bed and decided she did mind.

"Sue Ellen, Dex's sister, remember? We met downstairs one evening and at Waterhouse the next day?"

Rather wildly Tillie said: "Right, right, I do remember. You teach art and you believe Dexter murdered Liz."

Sue Ellen flamed to the roots of her silvery hair. "I have my reasons—"

"I'm sure you do." More awake now, Tillie realized she felt quite unwell. "But first I want to tell you that when I checked on Dex's studio last night—no wait, maybe it wasn't last night, I seem to have lost track of time— the door was unlocked. Unbelievable! I mean, what more clear invitation to steal his paintings?"

"I've never had anything to do with Dex's studio. I never go there and I've never had a key. Dex never trusted me to have one. Anyway, I've come to tell you something, I don't know why—"

"Because you know I value his work?"

"Maybe." Sue Ellen looked over her shoulder as though she feared someone might be listening at the door and hitched her chair closer. "Today I went to see Dex's lawyer."

"Lawyer?" Tillie's head was throbbing now. "How un-Dex like."

"Our parents insisted we have attorneys. I never asked why; now I realize they actually had some money and were deadly practical besides. I'm sure they *assigned* my brother the local attorney Don Wakeman. Ted wasn't in the picture then. My husband's a lawyer, you probably don't know—"

"Actually I do." Could she mention his Hoyt paintings to Sue Ellen? No, she decided, not even to his wife. Especially not to his wife.

"Anyway, I spoke to Wakeman today because I'm even more concerned about Dex's paintings than you."

"Of course you are." At last Tillie felt slightly humbled. "And?"

"But he gave me the brush-off."

"Why?"

"He said I have no claim to my brother's work. He pretty much told me to mind my own business."

Head throbbing, Tillie tried reaching for her robe. Something bad had happened—was it only last night? Evidently she'd been conked, a word from the comics she'd devoured as a child. But why? And why didn't anybody seem concerned? She located it at the foot of the bed, found a wad of Kleenex in the pocket, blew her nose pathetically, and tried to refocus on her guest.

"But you're his only kin."

"Not really. I'm his only sib in the USA. Our sister Tanya cut ties when she married and went to Canada in 1977. So yes, I'm kin, but I have zero claim to anything of Dex's because, as I just found out, he made a will—"

"Ultra un-Dex like."

"I'm as surprised as you and I've known him a lot longer."

Tillie heard reproach in her voice. For the first time she wondered whether Sue Ellen resented her having taken over her brother so completely this past week. Yet how could she not have monopolized him with a deadline to meet? Anyway, Sue Ellen and her brother weren't on speaking terms.

"Wakeman showed it to me and *my name wasn't in it.*"

"I find that astonishing," said Tillie truthfully.

"Don't get me wrong: Dex had no money, only his work. Which he knew I respected and loved. But obviously that didn't count with him because he left his paintings to someone who's no relation at all."

Me, thought Tillie for a split second before realizing that Hoyt had made his will before he'd ever heard of Matilda Roth Hamilton. "To whom then?"

"To Adam Quick."

Tillie's felt her jaw drop and didn't care.

"I know nothing about Quick except he used to be married to Liz Barker."

"I've been interviewing him for my article. He was your brother's first patron, you know."

"Patron? *I don't think so.* What he did was buy Dex on the cheap, promising to make him famous. What a fraud."

"He did buy thirteen paintings."

"Yes, at bargain-basement prices. I'll never understand why Dex left *him* the paintings and not me!" Sue Ellen sprang from her chair and headed for the door.

Reaching across the quilt with a moan, Tillie managed to catch her hand. "Don't leave. I have a theory."

Sue Ellen disengaged her hand, but she stayed put.

"I'm guessing Dex didn't leave you his paintings because most of them were of Liz Barker."

"Why would that matter?"

"Because you've always hated her."

"Really! How could you possibly know something like that? What an insane thing to say."

"I'm right, though, aren't I?"

"No comment."

142

"Worse, you suspected your brother of murdering her. He told me more than once how that killed—"

"*Killed—*"

"Bad word choice. Hurt him deeply."

"That's not good enough. Dex made his will a year ago when Liz was thoroughly alive."

Tillie clutched her throbbing head; she wanted to twist it off and toss it into the wastebasket. "Then look at it this way. Quick was the only one who believed in Dexter enough to actually buy his work. Dexter was grateful. Besides, he figured Quick would promote his paintings if only to increase the value of his own."

"Whatever. What's done is done, I don't plan to contest the will. But there's another reason I'm angry, *though you cannot use this in your article.*"

"I promise not to."

"You think I was a disloyal sister to Dex, but that's not true. For years I've paid his bills. It was me who kept him afloat."

Tillie collapsed back onto her pillows. *Both* Gages supporting Hoyt? Really, her brain couldn't handle all this! Ted had bought two paintings, but Sue Ellen had helped long-term. Had Hoyt discovered her charity, felt humiliated to be still dependent on his sister?

"I have no answers," said Tillie weakly. "I just know you 'mortally wounded' him by suspecting him of murder. He said it more than once."

Sue Ellen zipped up her down coat. "I had good reason. Dex and Liz go far back. He's always been crazy about her, but she was way too popular to notice him. But when she left Quick, he hoped she'd fly into his arms. Instead she married the local veterinarian who's more than twice her age. Besides, Dex had a touch of violence running through him—like that white streak in his hair. I remember once at Sandy Beach a boy was teasing Liz, splashing and ducking her. Dex grabbed him, flipped him and held his head underwater until Liz and I realized the kid was drowning and screamed our heads off."

Tillie closed her eyes. She needed Sue Ellen to leave. "I'm sorry about the will," she said. "As for Adam Quick, I think he has brains enough not to kill someone whose will benefits him."

"What do you know, Tillie! You've been here four days—"

Tillie opened one eye. "Five, actually," she said wearily. "Anyway, if you read mystery novels at all you know that the benefactor of a will is too obvious a suspect."

"*Who says he knew anything about it?*" flashed Sue Ellen and was gone.

CHAPTER THIRTY ONE

The guard unlocked the cell door and jerked a thumb over his shoulder. "Visitor."

Smitty had been dreaming of birthing a breach calf in a huge dark barn, his hands deep in the cow's hot uterus.

"Visitor? Who is it?"

"I just take you there, Doc."

Running a hand over his thinning hair, he followed the guard down a cold corridor. At the end he unlocked a door and motioned him into a small room. Immediately the stench smacked him in the face. Then he saw a chair and a plate glass window with louvered openings at mouth-level. The pane itself was scarred as though a generation of prisoners had tried to claw their way through it. A phone sat on a ledge below the window.

"I don't see anyone."

"You will. You got thirty minutes." A key grated behind him. Smitty pulled the chair forward and waited.

He didn't recognize the woman in black who entered the visitor's room, wrinkling her nose and pulling a handkerchief out of her purse.

"God, this place reeks,"—at least he guessed that's what she said. "So we talk through this?" She touched the visitors' phone as though it were contaminated. "Hello, Dr. Barker," she said. "What a foul hole."

Smitty had picked up the prisoners' phone. "Agreed, but I'm afraid I don't know you."

"Think back, a long way back. Cocktails at Sandy Beach, rather *too* many cocktails? Dance Club in the late Fifties? Boat rides in the Darschs' Criss Craft?"

Smitty peered more closely at the woman behind the scored glass. Late Fifties? Way before Liz, of course; just opening his practice in Mills Lake, eligible bachelor in town—as he'd soon learned. His brow cleared.

"Marianne Clark?"

"You *do* remember, how flattering. It's Marianne Price now; I married Steve Price."

Smitty nodded. "I remember Steve, nice guy."

"Was."

"Sorry to hear he's passed."

"And I'm sorry to see you behind bars, shocked's more like it. What's going on?"

"I don't want to go into it, Marianne. Write it off as a crazy mixup."

"It's more than crazy—it's insane. Look, I'm told we don't have much time so I've got to spit this out while my nerve's up. I've come to apologize."

Smitty shook his head and waited.

"A while back the police came to me with a pack of your wife's letters."

"Liz's letters?"

"Yes. They were looking for a letter she *hadn't* written, a letter that had been forged."

"Why did they come to you?"

"I worked for years as a handwriting analyst. And I was damn good." Smitty silent, she went on. "Well, I found a forged letter, all right. They'd given me letters of yours for comparison. I studied them for days before I handed in my verdict. I concluded that Liz hadn't written the letter in question *but you had.*"

The receiver dropped from Smitty's hand, hung there dangling like a man on the end of a rope. Finally he reeled up its cord, freckled hands trembling.

"I don't get it, Marianne. What the hell's this all about!"

"I'm trying to explain. *You're in jail because I went to the police and incriminated you.* But I've been going over my notes again and now I think you didn't write that letter after all. What's worse, I'm afraid I may have had a motive for pinning the letter on you."

Smitty shook his head in bewilderment.

"You rejected me, you know—way back then. You dumped me even though you knew I was crazy about you." She stared at the black leather purse in her lap, opening and closing the clasp. "Maybe I wanted to punish you for your indifference years ago, I don't know. But it's been driving me crazy."

Behind him a key cranked in the lock.

"They've come for me."

"Look, when I leave here I'm going straight to the police and tell them I was wrong. You'll be out of here tomorrow."

He laughed without smiling. "If only it were that simple. They've got a lot worse against me. But thanks for coming, Marianne."

CHAPTER THIRTY TWO

Smitty heard Nora before he saw her.

"All right, here's an ID. But if you think I'm stuffing this mink into a locker you're crazy. This coat and this purse I don't part with. And if you give me anymore flak I'll be on the phone to the State Prison supervisor. Yes, Litscher's a close friend of mine."

Two seconds later Nora in mink burst into the visitors' cubicle. "What fucking right do they have keeping you here!" But her belligerence died at the sight of Smitty slumped in a chair behind glass, defeated hands hanging between his knees.

He lifted his head, tried a smile that didn't go anywhere. "Don't swear, Nora, you know I hate it when you swear. It's gonna be all right, I'm fine. My lawyer's in touch."

"What lawyer is that?"

"Flanagan. I introduced you, remember?"

"Apparently I've forgotten." But she hadn't. A classic Irish beauty, Margaret Flanagan. Glossy dark hair swinging seductively whenever she moved her head. Cat-green eyes, white skin. She preferred not to think about M. Flanagan.

"She's good, you know. On top of her game."

"Which explains why you're still here."

"As you know, the mills of the law grind—"

"Exceedingly small. Except those are biblical mills and God wasn't in court the last time I looked. I repeat, why—"

"If you have to know, it's because the Madison police turned up a lethal dose of pentobarbital in Dexter Hoyt."

"Pento—?"

"The stuff vets use to put down big animals. I dispense it regularly all over Jefferson County, have for years." The phone slackened in his hand.

"I can't hear you, Smitty."

"I said, apparently it works with people too."

"Listen to me, you've got to fight this." Nora reached into her purse, took out a cigarette and lighter.

"You can't smoke in here, Nora."

"Really? I suppose I can't. Force of habit."

He noted inconsequentially that her nails were attractively lacquered. Liz had been a born sex-pot, though when he'd called her that she'd hooted. "*Sex pot*? Nobody says that anymore! God, Smitty, don't date yourself more than necessary!" But Nora was— he searched for the word—Nora was elegant. Understated, reserved, yet strong; stronger than Liz, he had to admit. He tore his mind from his dead wife, remembering he was trying to convince Nora he was optimistic about his release from prison. Though, hell, optimism was the last thing he felt. In his experience things could go wrong more easily than right.

"So it works with people—"

"Point is, Nora, who the fuck knows that except a veterinarian?"

"Don't swear, Smitty, I hate it when you swear." This time she was rewarded with a real smile. "But what about motive?" she pursued. "People don't kill without reason. How can the police think *you* murdered Hoyt?"

"I'll tell you how. When they searched my house they found something pretty damning. You probably don't know, but I had a few Hoyt paintings."

"I didn't know. I didn't know you were a fan."

"Unfortunately when the police barged in with a warrant they found them slashed to ribbons."

Nora's eyes widened. "I don't understand."

"Come on, I think you do. You being a psychiatrist and all."

With those words, she finally realized why Smitty had rejected her and married Liz Quick. *A psychiatrist and all.* To him "psychiatrist" meant a highly-educated doctor in a fancy office with a couch, making four times his salary by dubiously treating neurotic humans rather than sane dogs, cats, horses, and cows.

"But those painting were of Liz," she countered. "When you slashed them, you were symbolically killing your wife."

"Jesus, psychiatry! You're on the wrong track. I was not killing Liz, *I was destroying Hoyt's vision of her.* Even I know that

149

much about myself. I've always hated the way he painted her, even though I bought some of those paintings. Hell, maybe that's *why* I bought them, I dunno. Because when I was slashing them I honest-to-god felt I was finally killing his *possession* of her. Which has pretty much driven me nuts over the years. Liz felt it, you know." He shook his head. "I'm hopeless at explaining this kind of stuff."

Nora frowned. "But Smitty, who's to say *you* destroyed the paintings? What if Dex broke into your house one night—the police would believe that."

Smitty said sadly into the phone: "Nora, I *told* 'em I did it. Besides why in hell would Hoyt destroy his own paintings?"

"I can think of lots of reasons, starting with the fact that they're lousy."

Smitty didn't seem to hear. "Oh, yeah, and there's another thing. They've found an expert who says that a letter Liz supposedly wrote her sister was actually written by me. Forged." He had little faith in Marianne Price's pledge that she would go to the police and recant.

"I don't understand."

His chin dropped to his chest; he felt terminally tired. "I'm supposed to have forged a letter so no one would question Liz's absence last December."

Nora rose. She knew that if she didn't get out of there in three seconds she would start screaming.

"I've got to go, Smitty. Gigi's crossing four legs trying not to pee on the best rug." Realizing he couldn't hear her, she picked up the phone again.

"Tell me what to do. Smitty. Please."

"I don't know, dear Nora. Wait for those goddamn mills, I guess. *I* am."

CHAPTER THIRTY THREE

The Chief motioned Tillie to a chair. "I appreciate your coming in so soon after your unfortunate incident."

"I lost three days," said Tillie, sure that it would be weeks, even months, before she recovered from the "incident."

Sherpinsky leaned across her desk, brows question marks. She smelled of coffee and caramel and sweat. "Tell me what happened."

"*Well*," said Tillie, consulting the ceiling.

"From the beginning, if you can."

"It was my last day here, I was flying back to New York next morning. I spent hours finishing my Dexter Hoyt article"—Sherpinski nodded—"then remembered I hadn't walked Nora Klein's dog as often as I'd promised. I rang her and she told me to come over, though she'd be gone. But when I got there I couldn't find Gigi's leash—"

"Though Dr. Klein expected you—"

"I assumed she'd forgotten to hang it on its hook near the door."

"You eventually found it?"

"Yes, but by then it was so late that Gigi never got her walk." Tillie closed her eyes as though shuttering that afternoon at Nora's. Yet she knew there'd be more questions. Her head still hurt, her morale had sunk pretty much to zero. It was imperative, though, that the police get it right. "Then Nora came in. We said goodbye and I headed back to the Manse."

Sherpinski hunched forward. "Exactly when and where were you attacked?"

"It must have been going on six when I left Nora's, anyway it was quite dark. I walked up Coolidge then turned toward downtown and crossed Main."

Sherpinski nodded encouragingly; she was beginning to rather like Matilda Roth Hamilton.

151

"I passed the library, turned at the bank corner and started up Mulberry. Then all of a sudden I felt weirdly elated—excited, you know, I guess because my article was finished. I thought I heard music—"

"Moss, are you getting this down?"

Tillie whipped round, not having realized anyone else was in the room, and recognized the young officer who'd booked her in Hoyt's studio on a murder charge.

"This may be important. What kind of music?"

"It was that Roberta Flack song, you know, 'Killing Me Softly.' I figured it must be coming from a cafe or something."

"I can't think of a cafe nearby, can you, Moss?"

"I can't think of a cafe in the whole town."

"There's the Opera House bistro," objected Tillie, head now throbbing.

"True, but I don't think Opera House has music that you could hear blocks away. The town wouldn't put up with that. Check it out, though, Moss."

"On it, Chief."

"Did you see anyone, Ms. Hamilton? Pedestrians, cars—anything? This is important."

"I wouldn't have been dancing like an idiot if I had."

"Go on."

"So I was hearing the music and dancing and snow was falling. And then all of a sudden I felt a shock of pain and a snow bank came up to meet me. I remember thinking I'd never get up again. They took me to some hospital—"

"Fort Atkinson."

"Afterwards I was told that the City Manager had found me and carried me to the Manse."

"And then?"

Tears filled her eyes. "I'm so tired," she whispered.

Sherpinsky came round her desk and laid a kind hand on her shoulder. "Thank you, Ms. Hamilton, that's all for now. Sergeant Moss will drive you home."

CHAPTER THIRTY FOUR

"Matilda, what the hell's going on?" *Art World's* editor had discarded the cosmopolitan drawl. "Your Hoyt piece is seriously overdue."

"I know that, Mr. Jesko. But there have been serious developments her."

"What kind of developments?"

"I told you Dexter Hoyt was murdered."

"Did you? Oh, yes, I remember now."

Suddenly New York seemed to her far away and rather provincial. "I should also report that I was attacked and left for dead in a snow bank."

"Attacked and--? Matilda, your inflamed imagination has always been one of your flaws."

"If only it were imagination. Anyway, you'll have my article as soon as I complete it to my satisfaction." The knock on the head had accomplished one thing at least: she no believed her article was the most important thing in the world. "With, I'm happy to report, stunning photographs." When Ely had come by to hand over his work, she'd decided his photography was almost on a level with Hoyt's art. But even as she said the words, she felt detached, aching, weary.

Boycks flagged her down as she hung up.

"Wilk Steeves to see you." His voice suggested she'd soared in his estimation. Well, why not, thought Tillie. Professor Quick, the EMS, Sergeant Crosby, Sue Ellen Hoyt, now the City Manager.

"Where can I see him?"

"The parlor's for gentleman callers," winked Barry. Hadn't he said the same thing when Quick had visited her, could it have been only a week ago?

The Manse parlor still flaunted a faded Victorian glory, white-curtained windows illuminating half the large circular room, anchored by window seats. When she'd first seen it, Tillie had imagined a Victorian girl, hair tied in a blue ribbon, lying stomach down on the velvet pillows, chin in hands, small boots waving in the air, lost to the world as she devoured *Little Women*. A scowling Wilk Steeves stomping up and down in big snow boots did not fit this vision. He looked up.

"There you are! Hello!" he shouted, though she was quite near.

"Hello," she said carefully. Does he think I was struck deaf as well as half-dead?

"Is there someplace we can talk?"

She gestured at the empty room.

"Oh, right!" He looked around as though registering the parlor for the first time. "Fine! Do you have a minute?" He seemed abnormally emphatic.

She pointed to the largest chair in the room.

"This one's good for me." He sat down on a hassock but immediately his knees hit his chin. Tillie took charge.

"I prefer the hassock. Please, this chair is for you." She took the vacated footstool, crossed her ankles and looked attentive. Pain played a tattoo in her head.

"Yes, well. How are you feeling after your ordeal?"

"Post ordeal-ish."

"Of course! Bad experience, must have been."

"That describes it."

"I feel lucky to have come along when I did."

Tillie knew she should say "No, *I'm* the lucky one." Why couldn't she?

"I suppose the police have talked to you?"

"The chief interviewed me, with Sergeant Moss. Oh, and Sergeant Crosby, I guess he was what they call the first responder?"

"Actually Barry Boycks called 911. The EMS was here in minutes."

"Impressive."

"Do you remember the ride to hospital at all?"

"No. I do seem to remember some doctor with a red beard wearing green pajamas and a stethoscope around his neck. I think he questioned me."

"Then the ambulance brought you back to Mills Lake?"

"What is this, Mr. Steeves, an exam? Isn't it enough I went through it?"

Wilk flew up his hands. "You're right, of course. Anyway the EMS did not cart you back, I did. I'd followed the ambulance to Fort—felt personally responsible for you somehow—hung around to hear whether you'd live or die. Fairly happy to hear you'd live."

"Thank you."

"De nada." He ducked his head, a little proud of the phrase. "But as City Manager I do need to know these things. Community safety and all that. Do you have any memory of what led up to the attack? That seems crucial to me."

"Everything I remember I've already told the police."

"If it's not too much of an effort, could you fill me in as well?"

Tillie groaned. It *was* too much of an effort. Must she recap her ordeal once more?

"I left Nora's house after five, I guess. There was a brilliant sunset over the lake, I remember. I was walking back to the Manse, I like to walk—"

"I often feel the need myself."

"And was only a couple of blocks away when somebody conked me on the head. I don't remember anything after that. I'm told you saved me from freezing to death in the snow."

"Thank god I was there."

"So that's why you were out on a bitter cold February night, just stretching your legs?"

"That's it."

"Without Fletch?"

He smiled. "You remember his name. Yes, old Fletch had a run-in with the neighborhood Doberman. Nothing fatal, but he's still favoring a hind leg."

Plausible, thought Tillie. Yet she could not forget the creek, his "Pretty sure I'm in the clear, not a shred of evidence."

She wanted to trust him, but could not. Yet why was she a threat to him? Had she gotten too close to the truth about Liz

155

Barker's death? To Hoyt's? She shivered,. "Do you mind? I'm still not recovered."

"I understand."

In the front hall she extended her hand.

"I'm grateful for your checking up on me, Mr. Steeves."

He winced. "Wilk preferred."

She felt a little current shoot through her.

"As for saving my life, thanks can never be enough, can it."

She started up the grand staircase. When she paused on the landing to look over her shoulder, he was gone.

CHAPTER THIRTY FIVE

"I need to see Chief Sherpinski right away."

Sergeant Moss blew her nose; it was head-cold season. "So does everybody," she said, continuing her typing.

"But I *really* need to see her."

"So does everybody."

"I have important information and I'm leaving town tomorrow."

"So's everybody."

"Sergeant Moss, *help me.*"

The Chief greeted Tillie swallowing a yawn. All night the two murder cases had jumped like sheep over a fence as she'd vainly tried to herd them into order with a shepherd's crook. And now here was Ms. Hamilton perched on the edge of her chair obviously boiling with news. Sherpinski remembered when a busy day consisted of two parking tickets, one speeding citation and a seatbelt violation.

"How can I help you?"

"I think I may know who the murderer is."

Sherpinski reached for her coffee; it was dead cold. "What murder are we talking about here? Mills Lake's very busy these days."

Tillie frowned at the sarcasm. "Both murders, actually. I think there may be important clues in one of Dex's paintings." Now that he was gone she felt she could claim the intimacy of his nickname.

Sherpinski leaned back and chair springs groaned. She'd ride this out. "Which painting's that?"

"An abstract, which he just about never does. It was hanging on his studio wall. Then after his demise (lovely word, though somber) it was gone."

"Tell me about these clues."

Tillie hunched forward. "There're all there in the painting. First something that may be a boat, that's crucial. Then a white thing that could be a scarf or shawl or a large handkerchief or even a moon, I suppose. And a beetle, at least I *think* it's a beetle. And red slashes of paint. They all point to the murderer."

Sherpinski sighed. "Ms. Hamilton, MLPD is not an art department." But she felt herself relenting, if only from fatigue. When everything had been so completely nutty the past weeks, why not nutty plus? "So what's with this boat and white shawl?"

"And beetle, maybe." Tillie hitched her chair closer, trying to ignore her still-throbbing head. "All right, I'm guessing Hoyt was murdered because he knew who killed Liz Barker. Does that sound totally crazy?"

"No more crazy than anything else I've heard today. And the day is young."

"So he recorded his suspicion in this abstract still-life. I'm guessing each item is a clue to the identity of the murderer. May I explain?"

"Can you?"

"Take the boat. The police say Liz Barker's body went into the lake sometime in December. Nora Klein—you know her?"

"I know who she is."

"She has a boat."

Sherpinski sighed deeply. "So do half the residents of Mills Lake, myself included."

"I suppose that's true. Anyway, I wasn't sure about the white thing, but now I am. Because when I was looking for Gigi's leash in Nora's house yesterday, I found a white shawl."

"And the beetle?"

"That's less clear." Tillie frowned at her boots. "Beetles aren't generally harmful, but there is one—I looked it up—that's associated with death because it makes a sound like rosary beads clicking at a wake. And the painting's slashed with red and that could stand for blood."

Sherpinski studied the young woman opposite. Were these "clues" the residue of concussion? Finally she said, "Thank you for the report, Ms. Hamilton. And where is this painting now?"

"Unfortunately it's been burned in Nora Klein's fireplace, all but a bit of—oh, no!" She'd meant to take the charred frame with her, but she'd been unpleasantly surprised by Nora's return.

"So there *is* no painting, am I right?"

"I'm afraid so," said Tillie miserably. "But you'll look into it, won't you? *It's crucial."*

*****

The Chief had no intention of "looking into it." Then Moss came in with a sheaf of reports and laid them on her desk.

"Seems incriminating to me."

"What does?"

"Klein's burning the thing in her own fireplace."

"You've been eavesdropping."

"In this place you'd have to wear ear plugs *not* to."

It was mid-morning before she changed her mind. Ordinarily she would have sent Witter on such a mission, but the Captain was currently occupied with the increasingly active drug traffic in Mills Lake. So she sent tried-and-true Crosby. And Moss.

Crosby knocked on the Klein door, then pounded.

"Where is she, I wonder?"

"At the county jail with Dr. Barker, I'll bet."

"That's touching," sad Moss, fingering the silver loop in her nostril. How that ring had got by rigid police protocol she still hadn't figured out.

"I say let's bust in, we have a warrant."

"Cool with that," said Moss.

Inside, the house was silent.

"My god, look at this kitchen! I'm gonna have one like this someday."

Crosby groaned. Cops didn't make that kind of money, just ask him. He was also irate because he didn't expect to find anything here. Money protected you, like Marianne Price was protected in that fancy condo overlooking the Fish Hatchery. Some people seemed meant to have it, most people not.

They found no trace of a charred painting in the fireplace grate, though Sherpinski had warned them they wouldn't. It was past two before Crosby called to Moss from Nora Klein's office.

"We may have something here."

In an instant, Moss was breathing down his neck.

"Seems like a record of treatment." He passed a notebook to the irritating, sharp-nosed Moss.

She scanned the pages. "Jesus," she said at last, "I can't believe this! Know what this means?"

Crosby, always cautious. "I think I might."

CHAPTER THIRTY SIX

Again Tillie stood before the Chief's desk.

Sherpinski's face was unreadable, but she guessed she might be in trouble, wasting police time and money on a hunch. Barging into Mills Lake affairs. Questioning the MLPD's ability to solve crimes. She held her head higher.

Sherpinski wheeled round her chair and whispered to Moss at the next desk.

"You sure, Chief?"

"I'm sure."

Moss left and returned with a folder.

"You're leaving tomorrow, correct?"

"Correct."

"You understand that what I'm permitting you to see goes no farther?"

"No farther," said Tillie. *(But what about my article?)*

"You will speak about it to no one."

"I will speak about it to no one." Tillie had caught the beat.

"You have never seen this document."

"I have never seen this document."

Sherpinski nodded and left the room. Moss put the folder into Tillie's hands. The document that seemed to be a kind of medical record.

Case 513. February 10, 1980. Dr. Nora Klein, Psychiatrist, reporting. The case described below was brought to my attention by a colleague, Smith Barker. Though Dr. Barker is a veterinarian, I place a good deal of confidence in his analysis of human behavioral disorders, which are, of course, my expertise. As a result of Dr. Barker's urging, as well as my own interest, I have taken on Case 513.

Case 513 is a healthy, post-climacteric woman of fifty-six. Unlike many of my female patients, she is educated, financially independent, and of excellent standing in her professional field. Though her husband of twenty years died in an automobile accident in 1973, she appears to have successfully coped with widowhood. Again, unlike many of my female clients, she has transcended the stereotypical role of woman as (subordinate) wife, mother and homemaker. Though she and her husband were childless, she claims this fact did not negatively affect them; instead they relished the freedom to pursue their separate careers and share quality time with each other. In brief, 513 seems to be equipped emotionally, physically, and economically to lead a full and rewarding life.

After months of interviews, however, I have reached a different conclusion. I believe that Case 513 is a profoundly unhappy human being. One day in my office, for example, she revealed that she had taken early retirement because "certain personal issues" had begun to interfere with her client relationships.

When questioned about these "personal issues," 513 admitted that she had recently lost all sympathy with clients B and N and therefore the ability to help them psychologically. B and N were women whose husbands were involved in extra-marital affairs. 513 told me that their helpless passivity regarding their husbands' infidelities disgusted her. "Why do women just sit back and take it?" she fumed.

Eventually that question led 513 to examine her own behavior regarding marriage and infidelity. She was forced to admit that she had been "carrying a torch" for a married man for many years. As a result, she had a deep well of suppressed anger against both him and his wife, complicated by the fact that she had had sexual relations with this man while she was married. She had always thought of him as *hers* and was never able to adjust to the fact that he dropped her (now widowed) for a woman young enough to be his daughter. Her inability to accept the new reality tormented her; she began to have violent wish-fulfillment dreams. If only the new wife might somehow die, she and the man she loved could resume their relationship as before.

At the same time, as a psychiatrist, she was aware of the deadliness of her emotions. On the other hand, she deplored women's passivity. So that when she found herself alone in the office of the veterinarian she loved, she found it easy to slip into her purse a bottle of a lethal drug he'd left on his desk. After all, he'd always talked freely to her about his work — both the joy of curing animals and the sad inevitability of putting them to a swift and painless death.

Having stolen the drug, she found, however, that she could not go through with her plan, and hid the bottle on a shelf in her closet. Some time after, however, she changed her mind when she discovered veterinarian's wife was having an affair with a local attorney married to an art teacher who was her friend. Her anger reignited. Not only had the young wife taken the veterinarian from her, but was now betraying the man 513 loved.

She invited the wife for a drink in her solarium to watch the sun set (metaphorically so apt) and doped her drink. When she was unconscious, she injected the pentobarbital she'd stolen into a vein. Death was instantaneous. Hauling the body to her boat was a physical challenge but doable. Running without lights, she made for deep water where, with difficulty, she managed to tip the inexpertly-weighted body overboard.

To be clear, Case 513 had no idea that Dr. Barker would be charged with the deaths of both Elizabeth Barker and Dexter Hoyt. When she learned of his incarceration, she knew immediately she must tell the truth. She also confessed to forging a letter from the wife to her sister in Florida explaining why she couldn't make her annual Christmas visit. This was necessary so that no questions would be asked as to the wife's whereabouts. She did not for a moment think the letter would be attributed to the veterinarian.

Nor did Case 513 originally have any intention of eliminating Dexter Hoyt.

The page fell from Tillie's hand. She felt no surprise: she herself had urged the Chief to investigate Nora Klein. What she did feel was an enormous sadness. A great artist had been silenced because an otherwise intelligent woman had been corrupted by jealousy and passion. The second was regrettable; the first unforgivable.

She picked up the page and read on.

Case 513 barely knew Hoyt. Though surprised when he asked her to his studio for a drink, she accepted the invitation since she herself was keenly interested in art. She recognized immediately the subject of most of his paintings, yet found herself particularly drawn to an abstract in a black frame. When she

164

asked about it, Hoyt smiled. "I call it 'Guilt.' Most people would make nothing of it. I feel that *you*, however, could understand it very well."

With those words, Dexter Hoyt sealed his fate. If she had offered to buy the painting, his demands for money would never end. If she managed to steal it, he would paint it again. She remembered that she still had half a bottle of pentobarbital hidden away in a cupboard.

She trusts this confession will satisfy the local gendarmes of Smith Barker's innocence and result in his immediate release from jail.

As for Case 513, I have nothing more to say except: Physician, heal thyself.

CHAPTER THIRTY SEVEN

Bursting out of the police department, Tillie took the Municipal stairs two at a time. Again the curly grey head popped out of the office cubicle.

"May I help you?"

"*I have to see the City Manager.*"

"He's with someone at the moment. Name, please?"

"Doesn't matter." Tillie darted round the corner and sprinted down the long corridor. Skidding to a halt before his door, she paused to get her breath, head throbbing, then rapped once and opened the door. Steeves' head jerked up in surprise; his companion swiveled in his chair to see who was interrupting.

"Sorry, Mr. Steeves," gasped Tillie, "but I *must* talk to you."

Looking more bemused than angry, Steeves checked his watch. "I'm finished here in ten minutes. Surely whatever it is can wait that long?"

"It can't."

Steve leaned across his desk. "Sorry, Chet, this seems to be urgent. Let's get together before tonight's Council meeting, okay?"

"Not okay, but I'll be there." He also lowered his voice. "Who's the femme?"

"She's from New York."

"Encourage her to return." Newman brushed past Tillie, banging the door behind him.

Steeves' smile vanished. "What's this all about, Tillie?"

"Please, please can we take a walk? I have something to tell you."

"Can't you tell me here?"

She shook her head vehemently. "I can't."

Outside she steered him to the creek that foamed behind scrub trees and bushes. When they came to its bank, she caught her breath: Gigi's paw prints still dented the snow. Evidence, she thought wildly.

"It's time you tell me what's going on."

She looked into his perplexed—his handsome perplexed—face.

"Just this. I owe you an apology. One early morning last week I happened to be walking Gigi along this creek and I overheard you—I'm sure it was you. You said something terribly incriminating."

He pulled off the plaid cap, jabbed fingers through sandy hair.

"Look, New York, I've got a busy afternoon ahead—"

"No, please listen. I heard you utter these words and I quote: 'Pretty sure I'm in the clear. There's not a shred of evidence.'"

"*I* said that?" Steeves scrunched up his eyes trying to remember. "What did I mean?"

Tillie drew a deep breath; this was tough. "Since a Mills Lake woman had been very recently murdered, I thought the obvious."

He stared at her blankly; then, as her words sank in, recoiled as though she'd struck him. "Wait a minute. Are you saying—I don't believe this—*are you saying you thought I killed Liz Barker?*"

"I'm afraid that's exactly what I thought."

He shook his head sadly. "Tillie, Tillie, I'm disappointed in you."

"I don't blame you."

"I may know what you're talking about, it's coming back to me now. Would you happen to have any interest in the real story?"

"If it's true."

He ignored that. "One night last December I drove out onto the lake. Sure, I knew I was breaking the law because the lake hadn't officially been declared safe, but I also knew it *was* safe because I've fished it for years. I'd just cut a hole and sunk a line when I heard sirens. Holy shit, I thought: City Manager caught breaking the law, besides which I'd be slapped with a hefty fine. So I jumped into the Jimmy and gunned for the north end where there's a tricky little cove. Somehow I managed to ditch the cops, but I still felt kinda guilty about the whole thing. So the morning you're talking about—

I think—I said to Moss who was down at the creek grabbing her first but far from last smoke of the day and knows my ice-fishing mania, *I'm pretty sure I'm in the clear, there's not a shred of evidence against me.* At least you tell me that's what I said and I may have said it."

They'd turned away from the creek back to town. Now on East Lake they squared off, breaths smoking at each other in the cold.

"Fine," she said, wanting so much to believe it that that she hurt. "But that doesn't explain why you've been stalking me."

"*Stalking you?*" He raised his fists as though warding off another blow. "I give up, you're impossible!"

"I know it was you, Wilk. I felt it."

"*Stalking* you?"

"Yes, stalking."

"If you mean you were aware I followed you some nights— "

"So you did stalk me!"

"If that's what you choose to call it. I call it making sure you made it safely back to the Manse—"

She stopped and looked at him doubtfully.

"That's what I was doing, Matilda Roth Hamilton."

"Oh, do cut this Matilda Roth Hamilton nonsense!"

"Sorry, I thought that was how you address royalty. Anyway, I wanted to keep an eye on you. I was afraid your Hoyt research might have rubbed some local backs the wrong way."

They had crossed the Common and now headed up Mulberry, slogging through still another fall of snow. *Had* there been mulberries long ago? wondered Tillie inconsequentially. And had there ever been a Mills Lake February to rival this one?

"You really thought I might be in danger?"

'Yes."

"From whom?"

"Look, I'm not the police, just a concerned citizen."

"So that's what you were doing when you found me in the snow bank? Being concerned?"

"That's what I was doing."

They walked in silence, snow silting their shoulders.

"I know," said Tillie finally, "who murdered Liz Barker." She could not bear, yet, to mention Dexter Hoyt.

He stopped dead and looked about him as though trying to stabilize his position in the universe. "How can you?"

"The Chief traded that information for some important assistance I gave her."

"What assistance?" When she was silent, he shook his head. "You're not going to tell me, are you?" he said sadly. "You still don't trust me."

"I do, but I promised not to say a word to anyone. Oh!"— realizing she'd already broken half that promise.

"Relax, Tillie. I hope I'm not just anyone."

"You swear you won't tell anyone?"

"Solemnly do I swear."

She found that she believed him. "It was a confession written up as a psychiatrist's case evaluation. Only I soon recognized it must be a self-analysis."

"Are we talking about Nora Klein?"

"How could you know!"

"Just a guess: she's the only psychiatrist in town. But why would she incriminate herself like that?"

"Guilt, remorse, worn down by her secrets? I don't know. But I bet she hasn't flown the country or anything, I bet she's visiting Smitty Barker in jail."

"About that I have more than a feeling. I happen to know Barker's at home, released on Sherpinski's orders."

She spun toward him. *"Why do you always—"*

"Know everything? Relax, Tillie. As I've said, it's my job. Besides, you knew the big one."

One thing more was troubling her. "What will happen to Gigi?"

"That I *don't* know. I imagine Smitty'll see she's taken care of."

"Smitty? No! *I* want her."

"But you're leaving for New York tomorrow."

"Planes carry dogs."

They had reached the Manse. Tillie released the catch on the wrought-iron gate.

"This is crazy, but I have to ask. Did you send me a Valentine a couple of days ago?"

"Not to my knowledge."

She laughed. "Does that mean no?"

"Yes, it means no."

She would never really know.

"Well, goodbye, Wilk," she said, still not opening the gate. "I leave first thing tomorrow morning."

"I'm sorry to hear that. You *sure* you're well enough to travel? You look awfully pale. I'd say you're still hurting."

"I am, thanks for noticing." She wasn't looking at him, but there was something in her voice he'd been hoping to hear. She raised her head. "By the way," she said. "I hear you're from Chicago?"

"That's right."

"I've been wondering why you left the third biggest US city for a backwater like Mills Lake."

"Not quite sure. Getting rid of a three-hour commute every day? A chance to fish to my heart's content?"

"But such a big change. How could you adjust?"

He reached out and brushed a few snowflakes from her hair. "Someday, Tillie, I'd like to tell you."

"Someday I'd like to hear."

"Really?"

"Really, Wilk."

He tilted her face up to his, tenderly removed the rabbit-fur earmuffs, buried his fingers in her wild wet red hair.

Tillie felt a gush of warm spring water flooding her veins, her heart and her head. A rush of love dissolving the winter ice of fear and uncertainty, a rush of love melting all her doubts. She sighed a happy, gusty sigh.